S0-BDQ-589

ROOMS of the SOUL

ROOMS of the SOUL

Howard Schwartz

Illustrated by
Tsila Schwartz

CHAPPAQUA, NEW YORK

Library of Congress Cataloging in Publication Data

Schwartz, Howard, 1945-
  Rooms of the soul.

    I. Schwartz, Tsila, 1952-   II. Title.   III. Title:
Hasidic tales.
PS3569.C5657R6   1984   813'.54   84-8391
ISBN 0-940646-08-0 (Clothbound)
ISBN 0-940646-11-0 (Paperbound)

Published by: Rossel Books
              44 Dunbow Drive
              Chappaqua, NY 10514

AUTHOR'S NOTES

Hebrew terms appearing in italics throughout are defined precisely in the Glossary.

Although these tales are set in Buczacz, Poland about one hundred years ago, they are, in fact, tales of the present, disguised in the past, and what is more, they are, each in their own way, true.

By Howard Schwartz

Poetry
Vessels
Gathering the Sparks

Fiction
A Blessing Over Ashes
Lilith's Cave
Midrashim: Collected Jewish Parables
The Captive Soul of the Messiah: New Tales About Reb Nachman
Rooms of the Soul

Editor
Imperial Messages: One Hundred Modern Parables
Voices Within the Ark: The Modern Jewish Poets
Gates to the New City: A Treasury of Modern Jewish Tales
Elijah's Violin & Other Jewish Fairy Tales

IN MEMORY
OF RABBI ARNOLD ASHER

Among the Hasidim of Buczacz Reb Aharon ben Pinhas
was known as the Phoenix. So it had been for many years.
Finally one young Hasid asked Reb Zvi why this was. Reb
Zvi replied: "Reb Aharon lived from ashes to ashes, from
dust to dust, but he always rose up out of the ashes, like a
phoenix."

Acknowledgments

Some of these tales have previously appeared in the following magazines and newspapers: *Agada, Chariton Review, Fiction, Focus/ Midwest, Four Worlds Journal, The Jewish Post and Opinion, The Melton Journal, New Wilderness Review, The Reconstructionist, Reform Judaism, Response, River Styx,* and *The St. Louis Jewish Light.*

Some tales have also appeared in the following anthologies: *Gates to the New City: A Treasury of Modern Jewish Tales* (Avon Books) and *Sparks of Fire: Blake in a New Age* (North Atlantic Books).

"The Tale of the Rescued Torahs" is based on a true life story of Robert A. Cohn.

ROOMS OF THE SOUL

ROOMS of the SOUL

ROOMS OF THE SOUL

One *Motze Shabbat* the Hasidim of Reb Zvi gathered
around as Reb Naftali played the violin. While he played
the new melodies and set free the music that he heard
in the rooms of his soul, all of the Hasidim became caught
up in that music, until nothing else existed, for the music
absorbed all existence into itself. And out of this pour-
ing of the soul every one became connected to the
Shekhinah, who remained among them, even though
Havdalah had been already performed, and so too did
they reach a deeper understanding of the Scriptures,
which were illumined by the music. And during that time
they found their place at the center of the universe, and
there they made their home.

Then, while they were so caught up, Reb Hayim Elya
glanced up at Reb Zvi and received a great shock. For
the face of Reb Zvi had grown dark, as if he were
unmoved by the music. And that one glance at Reb Zvi's
face was such a shock for Hayim Elya that when he turned
back to the music the spell was broken, and the notes
of the music fell from his ears as if he had grown deaf.
Then Hayim Elya felt his soul sink. He felt as if he were

falling; the world began to grow dark. And in this way he descended from the heart of light into the heart of darkness, and all because of the look he had seen on Reb Zvi's face.

The next day, when they were alone, Hayim Elya approached Reb Zvi and told him of his experience the night before. Then he said: "Tell me, Rebbe, why was it that you were not caught up in the spell of the music, and what was it that caused me to fall so far in such a short time?"

Reb Zvi replied: "I was as caught up in the music as you were, Hayim Elya. I too saw the *Shekhinah*, the Divine Presence, descend from above and saw the waves of light reflected in her robe. And I too reached the heart of light that Reb Naftali led us to, and dwelled there."

Now Hayim Elya had great faith in Reb Zvi, but he found these words impossible to accept. And he said: "Forgive me, Rebbe, for having even a doubt of a doubt. But when I looked around the room last night as Reb Naftali played, there was a light shining from the face of every Hasid. But when I looked at your face there was no light to be seen. Tell me, for I must know—what was the meaning of that absence of light?"

Then Reb Zvi sighed and said: "What you are saying is true, Hayim Elya. For you see, so great is the power of Reb Naftali's music that it causes a man to pass through each of the rooms of his soul. Now in one of those rooms the *Shekhinah* flourishes in full glory, and that room is filled with light. You and I, Hayim Elya, reached that room first, and recognized the Divine Presence and received her blessing. And I, like you, hovered in that place like a dove above its nest, and left this world far behind me. But then I saw that there was another room next to that one, and that the door leading to it was open, and I understood that I must enter there. And even though I was reluctant to leave that place of glory, that heart of light, still I knew it was my destiny to explore every room. So, with great reluctance, I took my leave, and passed through the doorway into the next room."

"And what did you find there, Rebbe?" cried Hayim Elya, for he felt that a great mystery was about to be revealed.

And Reb Zvi said: "In that room, Hayim Elya, it was very dark. It took my eyes some time to adjust, after the great light of the *Shekhinah*. But at last I was able to make out a figure asleep on a bed. I drew closer and saw that it was a woman with long, dark hair. I had never seen her before, yet she was strangely familiar, as if her image had been sleeping inside me, in a room no one entered, long winters without waking; and the image of the moon was fading in her eyes. And when I looked upon the face of that woman, Hayim Elya, I felt my heart break, and all the light that I had carried into that room subsided, and I felt as if I were made of stone. Surely it was then that you glanced at my face. No doubt at that moment I pulled you into that room as well, but your eyes did not adjust to the darkness after that great light, and you saw nothing, but sensed the heart of darkness that you had reached."

When Hayim Elya heard this explanation he was silent for a long time, but at last he said: "Why is it, Rebbe, that this woman sleeps in a dark room beside that which is illumined by the light of the Sabbath Queen?"

And Reb Zvi replied: "Who can say why the world was made this way? All we can do is to recognize the truth as it exists—that the heart of light and the heart of darkness exist side by side, and that next to the room in which we are able to become caught up in the glory of creation there is another room of the soul which is dark, a cavern that does not admit any light, and woe be it if we should become lost there and not find again the doorway that can lead us to the other side!"

A PARTNER IN PARADISE

It happened in those days that word reached Buczacz
that a new *Tzaddik* had been proclaimed in Kotzk. And
this news shook the ground under the feet of all the
Hasidim who heard it, for this *Tzaddik* was a woman,
who was known as Tzaddika. And this Tzaddika travelled
around Poland and prayed with a small band of disciples,
all men, all Hasidim.

Among those stunned by this news when it reached
Buczacz was Reb Aharon ben Pinhas. And he was taken
with a great longing to find out for himself if such a thing
were possible. Then it happened that a copy of a Warsaw newspaper reached Buczacz, brought by a visitor,
and in this paper he read that this Tzaddika was to spend
the coming *Shabbos* at a *Beit Knesset*, a House of Prayer,
in Warsaw. So Reb Aharon took a carriage and travelled
to Warsaw, to the *Beit Knesset* where Tzaddika was to
stay. There he was welcomed as a guest by the Warsaw
Hasidim, many of whom had once made their homes in
Buczacz and still longed to return there.

During the time he spent in Warsaw awaiting the Sabbath, Reb Aharon was peaceful and calm, and he lived

in a state of bliss. He spent almost all of his time in the *Beit Midrash*, the House of Study, next to the *Beit Knesset*, sitting by the window and staring outside, for it looked out on a very beautiful place. And while he sat there a tale of the Baal Shem came to his mind again and again, though he could not fathom why.

So it was that the day Tzaddika arrived and entered the *Beit Midrash*, the first person she saw was Reb Aharon, staring out the window, with a smile on his face. Then she stopped abruptly and shrieked: "What do you think you are doing here!" And then Tzaddika began to curse as if she were in a rage, and her curses were more vulgar than even those uttered by men. The Hasidim of Warsaw were stunned by this behavior, but Tzaddika's Hasidim did not seem surprised. And Reb Aharon, he merely observed her, and the smile never left his face. Finally the old Hasidim of Warsaw turned and left the *Beit Midrash*, shocked and disgusted.

But when Tzaddika saw that her curses had not frightened Reb Aharon at all, she then began to whisper to him in the language of a harlot, trying to waken his lust. And when the younger Hasidim of Warsaw heard this language, they became ashamed, and they left the *Beit Midrash* in a hurry. But Reb Aharon only continued to smile.

Then the eyes of Tzaddika grew hard, and she began to sing Christian hymns, and made her Hasidim join in. At such a desecration the remaining Hasidim of Warsaw ran in a group from the *Beit Midrash*, holding their hands in front of their faces, so as not to look at this Lilith who had the temerity to call herself Tzaddika. Only Reb Aharon remained, though his face was now grave, and the smile was no longer to be seen.

Then the eyes of the demoness grew narrow, and she unleashed a great tirade against the Jews, and praised the tyrant Chmielnicki, whose pogroms had defiled the Jewish communities of Poland, and left men dead and women raped and everything burned to the ground. And when Reb Aharon heard her words he felt he had begun to sink into the earth, and he fell to the ground, and he began to weep a great weeping, as if all the griefs of the ages were crying out in him at the same time.

And one of the Hasidim of Tzaddika tried to console him, to stop him from falling into this great grief. But Reb Aharon recognized the man as a demon, as one of the murderers of his people, and he cursed him with a terrible curse, and the man limped away and fled from the *Beit Midrash*.

Then Reb Aharon felt like he was falling in space, but at last he came down to earth, and he fell as if into a sea of the tears he had wept. And in this sea he did not drown, but floated. Its currents carried him. And in this way he made his way back to shore.

Then, when he was able to sit up, he saw that Tzaddika, too, had been weeping. And Tzaddika now appeared very solemn, but the demonic aspect of her had disappeared. And she said, quietly: "I was sent here for you to tell me a tale."

At that moment the tale of the Baal Shem that had filled Reb Aharon's mind all the while he had been staring out the window came back to him. And he told her the tale of how, in a dream, the Baal Shem had seen his future neighbor in Paradise, and how he had sought him out, and found him unlike what he had expected, for he was very large and seemed devoted only to eating. Nor was he an especially pious man. Finally the Baal Shem asked him: 'Why do you eat so much?' And the man said: 'My own father, a God-fearing Jew, was tied to a tree during a pogrom and ordered to kiss a cross. When he refused they set him on fire, but because he was a thin man, the fire soon burned out. I, who witnessed this, vowed that I would never go out like a candle; I would burn so long they would never forget."

When she heard this tale Tzaddika began to weep once more. She wept for a long time, and when she stopped weeping she said: "Yes, this is the tale I came to hear. For I learned in a dream that in this place I would meet the one who is destined to be my partner in Paradise. And as soon as I entered here I felt that it was you; I knew by the divine aspect of your smile. But I had to be certain. That is why I blasphemed so terribly. Forgive me, but I had to know that you were a vessel that would not break before I entrusted my light to you."

And with that Tzaddika turned and left the *Beit Midrash*, and her Hasidim followed after her. Nor did Reb Aharon see her again all the days of his life.

THE THREE SOULS OF REB AHARON

In Memory of Rabbi Arnold Asher

Among the Hasidim of Buczacz there was none more beloved than Reb Aharon ben Pinhas. After his death at an age as early as that of Reb Nachman of Bratslav, it was said by many that he, like the Bratslaver, had been one of the *Lamed Vov*, the thirty-six Just Men who serve as the pillars on which the world stands. But he was not a simple man. He was a man who wrestled with his own soul as Jacob had wrestled with the Angel.

After Reb Aharon's death it became apparent that his mantle had passed to Reb Zvi. Reb Hayim Elya had been a Hasid of Reb Aharon. He had been in the Holy Land at the time Reb Aharon had died, and thus he had not been present at his funeral, which had been the largest in the history of the Jews of Buczacz, when there had been an outpouring of grief such as had never been seen before. (So it was said by all those who had been present.) When the news of Reb Aharon's death reached him, Reb Hayim Elya had been stricken like a man drowning. But then he had felt the soul of Reb Aharon lift him up from below and carry him to the heights. And after the time of mourning had passed, Reb Hayim Elya was among those Hasidim who came to Reb Zvi. For it is the custom among Hasidim to seek out a new Rebbe whenever theirs has passed away.

One night in a dream Reb Hayim Elya learned that Reb Aharon was one of those who had three souls. Although there may have been more to this dream message, that is all Hayim Elya remembered when he woke up. Puzzled, he went to Reb Zvi and asked him the meaning of the dream. When he heard this question Reb Zvi seemed to grow angry, and he told Hayim Elya: "Why have you come to me with this question? Let Reb Aharon answer this question himself!"

"But Rebbe," pleaded Hayim Elya, "Reb Aharon is dead. How is it possible to speak to the dead?"

"This is something you must find out for yourself," said Reb Zvi, and he turned away.

Reb Hayim Elya was confused as he left Reb Zvi's study, but by the time he had passed through the doorway of Reb Zvi's house he was already on his way to seek out Reb Aharon, as if it were still possible to go to that rebbe's house and find him there. That night Hayim Elya had a dream which came to haunt him for many days afterward. In the dream he found himself walking in an ancient city. The road he took in that city was round, and it was known that all those who started out on this road would one day meet all of the others who followed this path. And Hayim Elya could not tell if the city were Safed or Jerusalem, for it had qualities of both places, and yet at the same time was unlike either of them. But there was one thing in that dream that Hayim Elya was absolutely certain of—that if he continued on that path he would meet Reb Aharon.

Even in the dream, however, Hayim Elya had not forgotten that Reb Aharon was no longer among the living. And then the thought came to him that he might be walking in the City of the Dead. And this frightened him, for he was not certain how he might make his way back to the Land of the Living. And his fright caused him to cross from one world back to the other; and he woke up.

Remembering this dream, Reb Hayim Elya was distressed, for he had travelled that far to reach Reb Aharon and had lost his chance for a meeting because he had become frightened. And he was angry and disappointed, and anxious for another meeting to take place.

Then it happened the next day that there was a strange occurrence. A messenger arrived early in the morning, and delivered to Hayim Elya a letter from Reb Aharon, almost eleven months after his death. How was this possible? Reb Aharon had written the letter while he was still among the living, shortly before his death, but it had never been sent. Now it had been found among his papers, and delivered belatedly. And in the letter Reb Aharon answered the question that Hayim Elya had not asked until eleven months after his death. But this did not surprise Hayim Elya, for he believed that the Bratslaver had told the truth when he had said that a question may be asked in one time, in one place, and answered in another time, in another place. And in that letter Reb Aharon told the tale of how he had come to have three souls. And this is the tale that was written there:

"When the world was created, one Jewish *neshamah* was given to every Jew. But due to the tragedies that have plagued the Jews in every generation, from the destruction of the Temple to the pogroms of the tyrant Chimelnicki, the population of the Jews had become depleted, and now the number of living Jews was far less than the number of available Jewish souls. And for a *neshamah* to remain apart from a human being is to make it one of the Captive Souls, to deny its destiny to be born, like a flame that is forced to burn invisibly, even as it longs to reveal its myriad shapes and forms.

"So the angel Raziel was sent for by the King of the Kingdom of the Captive Souls, and given a message to deliver to the Holy One, blessed be He, a plea from the Captive Souls that their destinies might be fulfilled. And the Holy One heard their plea, and after that it became possible for a Jew to have more than one soul. And many were given a double portion, and became bearers of two souls. But to a very few of them, only the *Lamed Vov*, were bequeathed three souls. And it is both a blessing and a curse to be born with three souls. For so much abundance and so much responsibility is fraught with danger.

"Now it happened that I was one of these, cursed and blessed at the same time. For each of my souls was fully developed, each seeking to dominate the other; and each was so strong that together they nearly tore me apart. So my heart has become weakened. Of my three souls, one is the soul of the High Priest Aharon, brother of Moses; and one is the soul of Jacob, our Father; and the third one is the Angel with whom Jacob wrestled. And when this soul of Jacob would dominate over the Angel, my life was a great blessing and it was possible for the soul of Aharon to perform properly the duties of the High Priest. Yes, then it was as if the High Priest had been restored to the Temple, and the Temple rebuilt. But when the Angel held sway, the walls of the Temple were once more reduced to rubble.

"Now the soul of Jacob within me struggled endlessly with the Angel. Yet at times I hoped to come to terms with the Angel: I wanted to know what Angel it was—if it had been sent by the Messiah, the Prince of Light; or by the Prince of Darkness. Then I would meet the Angel face to face and look into its eyes, and I would fall under the Angel's spell. Thus I learned that the Angel lost its power over me if I did not meet its eyes. As long as I looked away I was safe. But sometimes my curiosity grew strong, and I wished to know what Angel this was, and I would meet the eyes of the Angel, and then it would hold sway until I could turn away once more.

"This is the lot that befalls every *Lamed Vov*, nor is it an accident. For the souls of the *Lamed Vov* must contend to keep the world in existence. For if pure peace should settle in the heart of even one of the *Lamed Vov Tzaddikim*, the world would sink beneath the weight of darkness. For the hearts of the *Lamed Vov* hold back the waters of the Abyss. And sometimes, when the pressure of the waters grows too great to bear, the heart of a *Lamed Vov* breaks."

Reb Hayim Elya read all the words of this letter in rapt amazement. Yet even more amazing to him was the fact that as soon as he had finished reading it the words and

letters began to dissolve, and soon disappeared. And then there was nothing left but dark powder on the white paper. And then Reb Hayim Elya woke up, and discovered that it was still the middle of the night, for he had fallen back to sleep and dreamed that a messenger had delivered a letter from Reb Aharon to him. And he knew that the meeting he had sought had indeed taken place. And he lay back on his bed and a light played around his face.

A SEA OF TEARS

It happened in the days after the unveiling of the stone of Reb Aharon and before the first *Yahrzeit* of his death, that Reb Zvi told Reb Hayim Elya a dream: "I dreamed that I was reading from the *Sefer* of one of my Rebbes. A dream of that Rebbe was recorded in that book. There he told how he had been submerged in a sea of Jewish tears and Jewish blood. And in the dream he did not want to come out of that place into *Gan Eden* as long as Jews were submerged in suffering.

"When I woke up the dream was still with me. And after I said the *Modeh Ani* prayer the first thing that came to my mind was the tale of how Reb Aharon had fallen into a sea of the tears he had shed over Jewish suffering. And I sensed that I had come close to a secret that had to be unravelled.

"At first it eluded me. But when I washed, and had poured water once over each of my hands, first the right, then the left, all at once I understood that there had been a mystical bond between Reb Aharon and my Rebbe.

"And when I had washed my hands for the second time, I understood that I had been one of the Hasidim of Reb Aharon, without ever knowing it.

"And when I washed for the third and last time, I understood that even after his death Reb Aharon was still grieving over the suffering of his people, as if he were submerged in a sea of tears."

A BEGGAR IN BUCZACZ

One morning Reb Hayim Elya entered the *Beit Knesset* in Buczacz for *Shahareis*, the morning prayers. And when he entered all the other Hasidim turned and stared at him with confusion on their faces. And Hayim Elya could not understand why. Then one of Reb Zvi's Hasidim came to him and said: "What is the matter with you, Hayim Elya? Why are you dressed that way?" And Hayim Elya looked down at his clothes and saw that he was wearing the rags of a beggar. And then he too was confused. For he had only risen from bed an hour before, washed and dressed and made his way in the dark to pray. And now, somehow, on the way through that darkness he had become a beggar, of the sort who never sleep under the same roof two nights in a row.

When Reb Zvi saw what was happening he left the place where he had been donning his *tefellin* and walked over to Hayim Elya and drew him aside, and said: "Come with me, Hayim Elya. I have been waiting for you to cast the husk aside and bite into the fruit." And Reb Zvi led Hayim Elya to the *bimah*. And it was then that Hayim Elya discovered that he could no longer *daven* from the *siddur*, for he could no longer read the Hebrew language. And he turned pale and whispered to Reb Zvi: "Rebbe, I can no longer read these words, the Hebrew is foreign to me. What shall I do?"

And Reb Zvi said: "Yes, Hayim Elya. I knew it was true the moment I saw you without your own clothes, dressed as a beggar. I knew that you had left your Hebrew in the same place you had left your clothes. No, Hayim Elya, this time you have been forced to leave everything behind, no matter how valuable it is in your eyes. For this is a journey that every man must make. But most men, like fools, only make it once, at the end of their lives. And you, Hayim Elya, have found a way to practice going empty-handed, and in this way you have discovered the secret of how to bring a rain of blessings to fill the cup of your empty hands. Do not be concerned with your knowledge or your appearance, Hayim Elya. While man sees what is before his eyes, God looks into the heart. Start the service!"

And Hayim Elya, although only a beggar, opened his mouth and sang, and the words rose up by themselves, even though they were foreign to him. And he saw them emerge as one who is a witness, and those who heard his voice that day knew they were hearing the voice of his Celestial Soul. For now that Hayim Elya had cast his clothing aside, his Celestial Soul had been set free. And those who heard him that day knew that at least once they had seen his soul not as a multitude of many sparks, but as a single flame.

REB HAYIM ELYA HAS A VISION

It happened in his thirty-second year that Reb Hayim Elya journeyed on his own to the Holy Land. In the end his journey was very fruitful, for there he met and married his wife, Tselya, who had been born in the Holy Land of parents who had come there from Baghdad.

But in its beginnings his journey had been very difficult. Reb Hayim Elya's ship had docked in Haifa. There he had gone into the town and spent the next twelve days in an inn beside the shore, while waiting for the carriage that would bring him to Jerusalem. Now Hayim Elya had always dreamed of being in *Eretz Yisrael*. In one recurrent dream he had seen the Holy Land from a distance, and it seemed to glow like a precious jewel. And in another he had stood beside a beautiful beach and watched the waves approach and depart.

But it happened that the inn was run by Arabs, and the innkeeper was hostile and suspicious, and the other guests unfriendly. Nor was there anything in that place that Hayim Elya could eat, and he subsisted on dry bread and water the whole time. But worst of all, the beach behind this inn was covered with ashes and littered with trash.

For each of the twelve days Reb Hayim Elya spent there in that place he was haunted by that black beach, so unlike the beaches he had imagined in his dreams of *Eretz Yisrael*, and all that time he felt as if his feet were sinking into the earth.

On the twelfth night, one day before the carriage was to depart, Reb Hayim Elya returned to his room, feeling sadder than he had ever felt in his life. And he put out the candle and lay down on the bed, and turned in the darkness in the direction of the one wall in that room which faced the shore outside.

But when he looked the wall had vanished, and the shore was illumined before his eyes. Nor was it the same shore he had suffered beside for twelve days, but another shore, far more beautiful than any he had ever seen. It was surrounded by a glowing light, unlike any other, as if it were the light of the first day of creation, before the sun and moon had been brought into being.

Reb Hayim Elya stared at that beautiful beach for several minutes. Then he realized that he was still in his room, and he became frightened and jumped up and lit the candle, and when he did the beach disappeared.

Afterward he recognized this beach as the very one he had dreamed about all the years he had spent in exile from *Eretz Yisrael*. And he knew that the Holy One, blessed be He, had opened his eyes and let him see the beach of the Holy Land that is hidden from the sight of most men, who see in it nothing more than a beach in disarray, covered with ashes.

THE CIRCULAR CITY

While in *Eretz Yisrael*, Reb Hayim Elya traveled to the Holy City of Safed, whose light is so pure it has been likened to the robe of the *Shekhinah*. He spent one day walking through the streets of Safed, which form a circle from the highest point of the city to the lowest, and back. Somehow it had happened that Hayim Elya was able to descend from the high place and return there without the effort or even the awareness of ascent. It simply happened that he found himself again at the starting point. Hayim Elya was much amazed to discover this.

When he returned to Buczacz, Hayim Elya described his journey to Reb Zvi. And when Hayim Elya had spoken of this strange quality of Safed, Reb Zvi replied: "You should know, Hayim Elya, that while the streets of Safed are circular, as you say, it is eminently easy to become lost there, and it is also possible to ascend and ascend without ever reaching the top. Few are those who make that steep ascent without even realizing it. That this happened is a sign that you have focused so thoroughly on ascent that you continue to do so even when you are not aware of it!''

THE TEST

One night Reb Hayim Elya dreamed that he and three other Hasidim of Reb Zvi came to the Rebbe and told him that they wanted to study Kabbalah. In the dream Reb Zvi agreed to teach them, and they came together on a certain day. But before they could begin their studies, Reb Zvi told them that they must immerse themselves in the pools; not only to cleanse their bodies, but also their spirits, and to relax, for their studies would begin with a difficult test.

Yet no sooner did Hayim Elya and the other Hasidim dive into the first pool than all the water drained out of it, and no sooner into the second than the same thing happened again. The time for the test had been set; it was irrevocable. And an anxious fear spread among the Hasidim as they traveled from pool to pool, for each time they submerged the waters quickly ebbed away.

It was almost time for the test when they arrived at the last pool, where Reb Zvi had agreed to meet them. They told him of their bad luck that day, and he pointed out that this last pool was not like the others, for it was fed by an underground spring, and he added that they should hurry, since the time for the test was at hand. And then, once more, Hayim Elya and all the others tore their robes from their bodies and prepared to dive in the water. But just as they did, Hayim Elya awoke, still uncertain if the water had received him or not.

This dream greatly perplexed Hayim Elya, and at the first opportunity he told Reb Zvi about it. Reb Zvi listened intently as Hayim Elya described the dream, and then he said: "The reason that you awoke before finding out what happened to the water in that last pool is because the results of the test are not yet known, for only now is the test to take place." Hayim Elya found these words enigmatic, nor they did not dispell the mystery for him. He said: "What test is this, Rebbe? For even in the dream I was not clear about what it was. And, in any case, how can one complete a test begun in a dream?"

Reb Zvi grew solemn when Hayim Elya said this, and he said: "Before I can reply to your questions, Hayim Elya, there is something I must ask you to do." Hayim Elya wondered greatly what this might be, and waited for Reb Zvi to continue. But Reb Zvi did not speak. He paused for the longest time, until Hayim Elya began to wonder if he were waiting for him to do or say something. At last Hayim Elya could not stand the silence any longer, and he said: "Please, Rebbe, tell me what it is that I must do. For I am willing to do whatever is necessary to put this test behind me." Then Reb Zvi replied: "I am sorry, Hayim Elya, but I am not permitted to tell you what it is that I need for you to do. Yet, at the same time, I must ask that you do it."

Now Hayim Elya was truly mystified. He cried out: "But Rebbe, that is as impossible to fulfill as was the demand of Nebuchadnezzar that Daniel not only interpret the meaning of his dream, but tell him the dream as well!" "Exactly," said Reb Zvi, "and did not Daniel tell him, in the end, all that he needed to know?" And with that Reb Zvi got up and left Hayim Elya alone.

All that day Hayim Elya wandered about in a daze. He could not conceive what was expected of him. He did not even know where to begin looking. Meanwhile his feet led him without being directed where to go, and by the end of the afternoon Hayim Elya found himself in the forest outside of Buczacz. In despair he sat down at the foot of a tree, and suddenly a great tiredness came over him, and he closed his eyes and fell asleep. And no sooner did this happen, than he began to dream.

In the dream Hayim Elya found himself standing at the foot of a mountain. The sides of the mountain towered above him, but somehow Hayim Elya knew that he must scale it. And even though he could not imagine ever reaching the summit, still he undertook to begin the ascent. And every step he took up that steep mountain required an amazing effort, but still he continued to climb. Nor did he ever look back, for he somehow knew that, like Lot's wife, he must not.

For what seemed to be hours Hayim Elya continued climbing there, although the light in that place never changed, as if it were frozen in the sky. At last he managed to scale the mountain and climbed upon its peak. Then, for the first time, he looked down, and there he saw the world from a great distance, not merely as it would appear from the top of a mountain, but as it would look from a much higher place, such as the moon.

It was then that Hayim Elya realized that he had in fact scaled the heavens and reached the moon, and the earth passed before him like a globe spinning far below. Hayim Elya was staggered, yet at the same time he knew he had ascended there for a purpose, and now he tried to remember what it was. He looked around the moonscape to see if it would remind him, and that is when he saw

212 5435

Hebrew letters lying scattered in the dust. Hayim Elya could scarcely believe his eyes. He bent down, and found that letters, forming words, were scattered everywhere at his feet. All at once, Hayim Elya realized why he had come to that place—to recover those scattered letters and words. And then, with a burst of strength such as he had never known, he set about to collect as many of those words and letters in his arms as he could hold, and he continued to gather them until he had completely filled his arms. And even so the number of words and letters that remained seemed infinite.

Still, Hayim Elya knew that he had done all that he could on that day. And when he picked up the last letter, the last word, that he could hold, he suddenly awoke, and found himself seated at the foot of that same tree where he had fallen asleep. Leaves had fallen from that tree and filled his arms, even as had the words and letters in the dream. And when Hayim Elya recalled this dream, he felt greatly strengthed, and jumped up and ran back to Buczacz, directly to the house of Reb Zvi.

And when he reached the door, he found that it was open, and that Reb Zvi was standing there, a wonderful smile on his face. And Reb Zvi said: "Sometimes words intended for us from on high become diverted and are lost for a long time. Then it is only the great efforts of one man, willing to go to any lengths, even to the beyond, who can restore them. And for this, Hayim Elya, I will always be grateful to you."

REB HAYIM ELYA GOES ON A MISSION

One day Reb Zvi took Reb Hayim Elya aside and spoke to him in his study. While Reb Zvi leaned against his study stand he asked Hayim Elya, his scribe, to travel to the nearby city of Kotzk to bring back a rare edition of the *Sefer Yetzirah*. This book was in the possession of a Hasid who lived there, who had brought it back from the Holy Land, and was now giving it as a gift to Reb Zvi. Hayim Elya readily agreed to undertake this journey, and Reb Zvi thanked him and told him to be certain to have the man inscribe the book for him.

Hayim Elya set out at once, in order to reach Kotzk and to return that same day. But only after he had left Buczacz and was well on his way did he realize that he did not know where in Kotzk this Hasid lived. And since he did not want to lose time by turning back, he searched for a sign from Heaven that could help him. And soon he became aware of the sound of carriage wheels ahead of his own, and when he pressed his horses he was able, at last, to come close enough to see this carriage that flew so swiftly ahead of his own. And there was something strange about that carriage, for it was pure white, and the upper portion of the carriage and the lower portion were fused to form a very beautiful balance, and it seemed to be surrounded by a glowing aura like that of a flame. And at one point, when Hayim Elya's carriage came as close as it ever managed to come to this elusive carriage, it appeared to him that it was travelling so swiftly that its wheels did not touch the ground.

By this time Hayim Elya had decided to follow this carriage, and so he let it lead him through that forest, across a bridge that ran above a river, and then out in the open across the fields that wound slowly away from the forest. So it was that in this way he came to find himself before the *Beit Knesset* in Kotzk.

But when Hayim Elya arrived at that House of Prayer there was no trace to be found of the carriage that had travelled ahead of his own. Then Hayim Elya entered the House of Prayer and asked the first Hasid he met about the way to the home of the one he was seeking, for he had not forgotten the purpose of his journey. And it happened that this Hasid was in the *Beit Midrash* next door at that very moment, and, by chance, he had with him the very book Hayim Elya had journeyed for, since he had brought it that day to show to the Hasidim of that *Beit Midrash*. Then, without Hayim Elya's having to ask, the Hasid gladly inscribed the book as a gift to Reb Zvi, and asked Hayim Elya to deliver his blessings to the Rebbe as well. And Hayim Elya thanked the man with all his heart and took his leave.

Night was falling as Hayim Elya reached Buczacz, and he went directly to the *Beit Knesset*, where he knew he would find Reb Zvi. He entered there just as the Hasidim began to pray *Ma'ariv*, the evening prayer, and the first words he heard as he stepped inside were "*Barchu es Adonai hamevorach*," "Bless the Lord who is to be blessed." And when Hayim Elya heard those words, he knew that his mission had succeeded.

After the service had ended Reb Zvi called Hayim Elya aside and his face was glowing. Without a word Hayim Elya took out the book from beneath his coat and gave it to Reb Zvi. And Reb Zvi smiled as he received it and said: "*Baruch HaShem*, Bless the Name. I am very grateful for this, Hayim Elya, more than you might realize. But tell me, why did it take you so long to catch up with my carriage?"

DOCTOR BESHT

In Buczacz there was a woman whose *neshamah* had a mystical bond to that of Reb Zvi. One night this woman dreamed that both her children, a boy and a girl, were suffering from an affliction. She did not know what it was, and in the dream she went to Reb Zvi for advice. He told her to go to see Doctor Besht. This she agreed to do, and she was on the way to consult with Doctor Besht when she was awakened by the crying of her daughter, who at that moment was having a nightmare.

Later that day this woman came to Reb Zvi and told him her dream. "Certainly," Reb Zvi said, "if the message was meant to be delivered from the Besht, the child would not have awakened you from your dream. For Duma, the angel of dreams, would not contradict himself. He would not send a dream to interrupt a dream unless it was intended to end. Furthermore, the crying of the child at that very moment confirms your dream. I suggest you take down the book *Shivhei ha-Besht* and opened it at random and read the first tale you come to, and take it to your heart."

And the woman did as Reb Zvi said and opened the

book at random to the tale of a child who suffered for lack of love. She reported this to Reb Zvi, who told her that she must find it in herself to express the love she felt for her children. This the woman did, and before long her children blossomed and became healthy in body and soul.

REB ZVI'S ABSENCE

One year it happened that within one week two Jewish couples in Buczacz gave birth to twin sons. Just as remarkable was the fact that in both cases Reb Zvi had participated in the conversion of one of the spouses—in one case the husband, and in the other, the wife. Then it happened that Reb Zvi was urgently called out of Buczacz and therefore missed both *Brit*s, which took place on successive days.

On his return Reb Hayim Elya asked Reb Zvi: "How is it possible that you, who were responsible for restoring the *neshamah*s of these couples to Zion, were absent in both cases from the Covenant of their offspring which made them one with their Creator?"

And Reb Zvi said: "Although you and the others did not see me, Hayim Elya, I was still present at the signing of the Covenant. Let me explain. There are two stages in any contract—the first signing to certify that an agreement has been reached, and then the receipt given on completion of the agreement, which shows that what was promised has in fact been given and received.

"As you have said, Hayim Elya, I was present at the

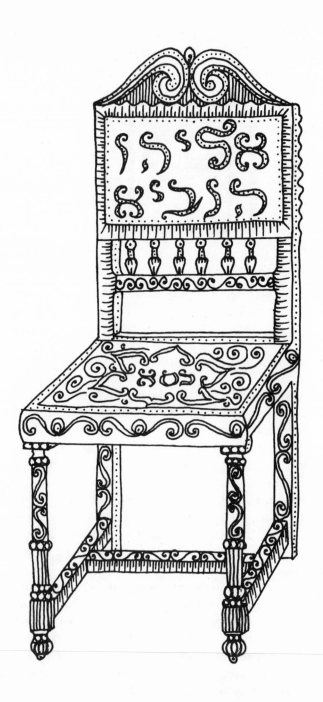

Covenant that restored the *neshamah*s of the husband in one case and of the wife in the other. Therefore it was required that I be present at the Covenant of their offspring. That is why I said I had been called out of Buczacz. In fact, my body rested in my study while my *neshamah* threaded its way to Paradise. There I was present when the angel Metatron announced that both sons of both couples had received the complete Covenant, and I saw the Divine Name written on the Seal, and the Seal pressed to the parchment. And after Metatron and each of the angels, it was my honor to sign the documents and to serve as the witness from this world. But please, Hayim Elya, do not ask me to reveal any more about this."

Reb Hayim Elya was amazed to hear what Reb Zvi had said. For he had not forgotten the four sages of the Talmud who had entered Paradise, and how fraught with danger was such an ascent. Of the four, Ben Azzai had looked and died; Ben Zoma had looked and lost his mind; and Elisha ben Abuyah had "cut the shoots" and become an apostate. Only Rabbi Akiba had ascended in peace and descended in peace. And Hayim Elya was drawn towards the lowest stairs of the ladder that must be climbed to make such an ascent, but he could see that Reb Zvi would say no more about it. Therefore Hayim Elya raised another question that was on his mind: "Tell me, Rebbe, why is it that although the twins of the first couple were born seven days before the second twins, it was the second twin sons who were circumsized first, by one day, since the first twin sons were weak when they were born, since they were premature?"

And Reb Zvi said: "These twins, as you have guessed, Hayim Elya, have mystical links between them. For the firstborn son of the first couple shares his *Nekevah* with the second son of the second couple, while the remaining sons have *Nekevah*s that are likewise linked. And together these four infants have much to accomplish, for there are many Wandering Souls who depend on them to complete their work in this world. The first pair to be born deserve special consideration, but the first to be circumsized also receive special consideration. Therefore the honors are even and the links are revealed to be as intricate and balanced as *pilpul*. These children, Hayim Elya, are truly blessed.''

THE GATES OF *PARDES*

It was acknowledged by all that Reb Shalom of Jerusalem was the greatest kabbalist of his time. In his hands mystic words yielded secret meanings the way the fountain spouted forth from the rock when Moses struck it with his staff. So too could he understand the secrets of the Sefirot as if they were doors that sprang open at his touch.

Rumor also had it that Reb Shalom had in his possession a manuscript of the lost book *Sefer Pardes*, which Moses de Leon was said to have written in the Thirteenth Century. It had long been believed that in that book was not only to be found the secret of how to call down the *Merkevah*, the Divine Chariot, but also how to ascend into the heavens within it. So too was it rumored that Reb Shalom himself had once entered *Pardes*, and like Rabbi Akiba before him, had departed in peace.

For many decades other Hasidim had made a pilgrimage to the home of Reb Shalom in Jerusalem, in hope of being permitted a glimpse into this book. But while Reb Shalom was more than willing to show them his immense library of kabbalistic books and manuscripts, that one manuscript he never took out or showed to anyone. In fact, those who had dared to ask him if he had the book in his possession received no satisfaction, for he always said that he could not reply to that one question.

Now when Reb Hayim Elya of Buczacz set out for the Holy Land, he carried with him many letters to be delivered. For it happened that every rebbe in Buczacz had written a letter to Reb Shalom, all of which Hayim Elya dutifully delivered to him. And when Reb Shalom saw that collection of letters, he treated Hayim Elya like the king's messenger, and spoke with him at length, asking him of everyone and their families. For many of them had visited him in the Holy Land, and he too had traveled through all of Poland and Russia more than once in his long and fruitful life.

At last Hayim Elya was able to ask Reb Shalom some questions about Kabbalah, which he had prepared in advance, for he knew that he might never again have the opportunity to speak with such a master of the Divine Mysteries. And Reb Shalom replied to each question directly, with simplicity and clarity, as if it were not the most arcane mysteries of which he spoke, but the most obvious facts. And in one hour Hayim Elya learned more of the secrets of the Kabbalah than had ever been revealed to him in all of the days of his life. So clear did his vision become that Hayim Elya felt that he could step through the gates of *Pardes* then and there, were he to know where to find them.

Then it happened that Hayim Elya was suddenly possessed by a deep longing to look upon the pages of the legendary *Sefer Pardes*, for he felt that should he gaze upon them, any letter would lead him directly to *Pardes*. And in that moment Hayim Elya could not restrain himself, and asked Reb Shalom if he might, indeed, permit him a single glance into the pages of that book. Reb Shalom was completely taken aback at first, and for a long moment he stared at Hayim Elya in stunned silence. Then to the utter amazement of Hayim Elya, he said: "Yes. I will permit you to read in it, for I sense your longing to pass beyond those gates. But I no longer have the book in my possession. If you want it you must go to Reb

Menachem in Warsaw, for it is he to whom I have entrusted it—for I am old, and I do not want the book to fall into the wrong hands. But if you travel to Warsaw and find Reb Menachem, you may tell him that I sent you. And he will believe you, because I will give you a letter to show him. And besides, no one else knows that he has the book in his possession.''

Hayim Elya listened to these words in complete amazement, and the curtain before *Pardes* shimmered in his vision and almost parted then and there. But in the end it still remained closed to him, and he knew that it would not open until he had reached Reb Menachem and gazed upon the pages of that book. Yet Hayim Elya knew that without the blessing of Reb Shalom it might never open to him, and its mysteries would remain hidden from him for all time. For it is only the destiny of a few to look upon the treasures of *Pardes*, such as the eternal lamps of which Reb Nachman sometimes spoke, that glow eternally, or the key that unlocked a thousand worlds, or the golden feather of the golden dove of the Messiah, which the Baal Shem almost touched. And if he had, the age of the Messiah might be upon us even now.

Just contemplating these treasures, Hayim Elya seemed to waver at a great height, as if the heavens were once again calling him closer. But at last he put all those shimmering mirages behind him, and found himself in the presence of Reb Shalom, and understood at once that it was he who had opened all those doors of possibility to him, which he had never even known had existed. And Hayim Elya was grateful to the root of his being, although he had no way of expressing this. Yet he saw that Reb Shalom recognized it, and he understood how he had been rewarded by his generosity.

Then Hayim Elya took his leave of Reb Shalom, whom he did not see again in this lifetime. For less than two years later Reb Shalom departed from this world and took his place among the righteous in the World to come. But long before then Hayim Elya had returned to the fields of Poland. And even before he returned to Buczacz, he set out at once to find Reb Menachem in Warsaw. For the long lost pages of the *Sefer Pardes* shimmered in his imagination as if they were written with fire, and he knew that he would never rest until he had sought them out.

Now, if the truth be known, Hayim Elya was a reluctant traveler. He preferred to stay in the House of Study, immersed in the sacred texts, caught up in the questions of the Torah. But in this instance he set out like an Israelite in search of the Promised Land. In this way he at last reached the city of Warsaw, which was far larger than any city he had ever seen. Lost in the complexities of that city and its many by-ways, Hayim Elya tried to follow the path that he had been told would lead to Reb Menachem. But by mistake he took the wrong road, and left the Jewish Quarter and found himself in an area of the city where Jews were never seen, for they dared not show themselves, so vicious were those inhabitants. And there Hayim Elya walked, in his dark robe, for all the world to see. Yet no matter where he walked, he did not see a single soul. For that day, miraculously, all of the Gentiles had gathered in their churches, since it was one of their holy days. And when at last Hayim Elya was sighted by a righteous gentile, he warned him at once to flee, and directed him back to the Jewish Quarter.

When Hayim Elya finally reached the street of Reb Menachem and approached his house, Reb Menachem, who saw him coming, came out of his home to greet him. And while they stood together before the door, Hayim Elya told Reb Menachem of all that had happened, and about how he had become lost on his way to his home. And when he heard this, Reb Menachem grew pale and said: "The last Hasid who made the error you speak of did not return to the Jewish quarter alive. Surely you have walked through the valley of the shadow. Whatever it is that has brought you here, I will surely do all I can to assist you. Come in."

Then Hayim Elya walked through the doorway, and no sooner had he stepped across the threshold than he saw the study stand of Reb Menachem, which was not far from the door. And open on the stand was an ancient manuscript, which Reb Menachem had been studying.

And when Hayim Elya looked upon those open pages he knew at once that they must belong to the *Sefer Pardes*, which he had come so far to find. And at that very instant the gates of *Pardes* opened to him, and he stepped inside.

THE TALE OF THE AMULET

In Memory of Rose Rubin

After the passing of his grandmother, Rayzel, Reb Hayim Elya inherited the library of sacred books that had belonged to his grandfather, Reb Zev ben Simha Leib, who had died ten years before. Among these books there was one very old leather-bound volume of the *Sefer Raziel*, written by hand, and Hayim Elya recognized at once that this was the jewel in his grandfather's library.

Then it happened that as Hayim Elya leafed through the pages of that book, a small parchment fell from it onto the table. And that parchment was worn and faded, and it was difficult to make out the text which was inscribed within the shape of a flame. And Hayim Elya was filled with curiousity when he saw it, and when he picked it up and studied it he had a very strange sensation, for it seemed to stir his spirit and waken his soul.

It took Hayim Elya several hours, but at last he succeeded in deciphering the words of the text written there. And this is the text he transcribed:

Master of the Universe, may it be Thy will that I gaze
upon the heavenly heights. Open for me all of the gates
of *Pardes*: the gate of *Peshat*, the gate of *Remez*, the gate
of *Drash*, the gate of *Sod*. May the gates of heaven open
to receive me that I may feed upon the radiance of the
Shekhinah and enter into each and every heavenly palace.
O, open now my lips that I may utter a song before the
Throne of Your glory. May it be thy will that I gaze upon
the flames of the Pargod, upon the black flames of days
of yore, upon the white flames of days to come (may they
be for a blessing!). Let me see each generation and its
interpreters as did the first man, and let me read in the
Book of the generations of Adam. And may I be found
worthy to taste its taste, which is like honey for
sweetness, as did Ezekiel the Prophet.

When Reb Hayim Elya had finally deciphered this text,
he realized that the parchment must have belonged to
an amulet, and that the amulet must have had a magical
purpose, although he was not certain what it was. Then
Hayim Elya showed the parchment to Tselya, his wife,
and even though she was a *sopher*, she had never seen
a similar design, and also wondered at its purpose. Then
they decided that they would go together to Reb Zvi, to
see if he could identify the amulet.

Now Reb Zvi was not surprised to see Hayim Elya and
Tselya and their child that day. For the night before he
had dreamed that Hayim Elya had pointed out a passage
to him in the Bible, and when he had awakened, he had
recalled it, and marked that place. But Reb Zvi had not
expected anything like the parchment, which he recognized at once, although he had never before seen one like
it. And what purpose did that amulet serve? For every
amulet has a specific function, either to ward off demons
like Lilith and the effects of the Evil Eye, or to be used
for magical purposes. And Reb Zvi recognized at once
that the parchment had been the text of an amulet that
had been used to gain entry to *Pardes*, the upper realms,
as Enoch did in his generation, and Rabbi Akiba in his.
For with the protection of the amulet it was possible to
ascend and descend in peace, as Akiba had.

Then Reb Zvi said: "This parchment, Hayim Elya,
belonged to an amulet that was once used for purposes

of the mystical ascent. For he who wore the amulet in which this parchment was contained would shortly be taken up into Paradise.''

And Hayim Elya asked: ''But how did this ascent take place?''

And Reb Zvi replied: ''There are many possible paths. One can be taken up in the *Merkevah*, the Divine Chariot, as was Enoch; or ascend the ladder that reaches from earth to Heaven, on which Jacob saw angels ascending and descending; or be transported to that place by means of the power of the Name. But in each and every case it is only the potency of the incantation inscribed on this parchment, contained within the amulet, that can protect those who ascend from among the living.''

When Hayim Elya heard this, he was filled with longing to make that ascent, for he was one of those who are drawn like a moth to the flame that burns eternally in Paradise. And Reb Zvi read all this in his face, and he said: ''Do not be deceived, Hayim Elya. This parchment cannot provide ascent by any of those paths.''

''But why not, Rebbe,'' Hayim Elya pleaded, ''I am certain it is authentic.''

''That is true,'' said Reb Zvi, ''But the parchment by itself is powerless. It cannot release its power unless it is accompanied by the same amulet for which it was written, for no other could ever work. No, Hayim Elya, that way is blocked to you, and an angel guards it with a flaming sword that turns in every direction. But do not despair—for there is still another path.''

''What is it, Rebbe?'' begged Hayim Elya, who had almost abandoned hope.

Then Reb Zvi said: ''This path is hinted at in the parchment, in the words 'let me taste of its sweetness as did Ezekiel.' And what does this refer to? You answered this question for me last night, Hayim Elya, in a dream. In the dream you brought me the *Tanach* and asked me to explain a passage in the *Sefer Ezekiel*.''

''Tell me, Rebbe, what was that passage?'' asked Hayim Elya, ''for I do recall speaking to you in a dream last night, but I have forgotten what we said.''

''Listen, Hayim Elya,'' said Reb Zvi, opening the Bible

to the place he had marked. "This is the passage you pointed out:"

> And when I looked, behold, a hand
> was put forth unto me;
> and, lo, a scroll of a Book was therein;
> and He spread it before me,
> and it was written without and within.
>
> And he said unto me: 'Son of Man,
> eat this which thou findest;
> eat this scroll, and go, speak unto
> the House of Israel.
>
> Then did I eat it; and it was in my
> mouth as honey for sweetness.

Then it happened that just as Reb Zvi finished reading this passage, Sharya, the infant daughter of Reb Hayim Elya and Tselya, crawled up to that table and took the parchment in her hand and brought it to her mouth. And when Reb Zvi and Hayim Elya saw this, both of them understood it was a sign, and at that moment Hayim Elya realized what must be done, which had already been apparent to Reb Zvi. And Hayim Elya said: "Now I know that I must eat this parchment, as Ezekiel ate that scroll."

And when Reb Zvi saw that Hayim Elya understood, he handed the parchment to him and said: "Yes, take this parchment, Hayim Elya, and pronounce the blessings over both wine and bread, and eat."

But Hayim Elya did not fully understand this command. And he hesitated and said: "But why both blessings, Rebbe? Why not only the blessing over bread?"

And Reb Zvi replied: "The blessing over bread serves only to bless the parchment; the second blessing serves to bless the ink as well. For the blessing over wine will transform the letters of the words into rivers that will flow from within, and the blessing over bread will make the words nourishing in your sight. Furthermore, if you only pronounced one blessing, and not both, there could be the danger that you would succeed in the ascent, but might not be able to return to this world."

Then Reb Hayim Elya pronounced the blessings over

רבון כל
העולמים
יהי רצון מלפניך שואפה
בזכותי שהיא פתח לי כל
שערי פרנסה: שער הפשט, שער
הרמז שער הדרש ושער הסוד.
ותפתחו שערי השמים לקבלני שואהיה
נזון בזיו השכינה אנכם לכל היכל והיכל
ותהא נא את שופתי ואהגה שירה לפני
נסא כבודך. יהי רצון שואעפה צלהבות
הפירגוד צלהבות השחורות של ימים
עברו וצלהבות הלצעות
של הימים הבאים עלינו לטובה
מי יתן ואראא כל דור ודורשיו.
ואקרא בספר תולדות אדם ואהגה
לטעות בפי לטעלמו שהוא בדצש
לאותק בפי שעשה יחזקאל הנביא

wine and bread, and he ate the parchment, and it was like the honey of manna to his taste, and he felt the rivers of words begin to flow. And in the vision that took form before his eyes, he saw the scroll of the Book that had been revealed to Ezekiel, and the scroll was unrolled, and the letters of that scroll burned like flames, black fire on white. And Hayim Elya read out loud the words that were written there without and within, and Reb Zvi, who shared in this vision, witnessing the scroll and hearing the words that Hayim Elya spoke, took down those words so that a record would exist in this world.

And in the black fire of the letters Hayim Elya read the history of his family, from the days of Abraham until that time. And in the white fire he read the future, until the End of Days. And when he looked up at last, he was amazed and terrified to discover that he had ascended to a very high place, and was hovering there, like a dove above its nest. And before him shimmered a vision more vivid than anything he had ever seen in his life. For there he saw the Celestial Temple that exists in Paradise, which is torn down and rebuilt every day as a reminder of the destruction of the earthly Temple in Jerusalem. And Hayim Elya saw the Celestial Temple reconstructed in his sight, from the first cornerstone until the final stone was in place. And when he gazed upon the splendor of the Temple in all its glory, he knew that his soul had been numbered among the blessed. But at the same time he began to fear that the splendor was more than a man may gaze upon and live, and he shut his eyes.

When he opened his eyes again, Reb Hayim Elya found himself standing beside Reb Zvi and Tselya, and realized that he had never stopped speaking during the whole of the vision, for he had never stopped reading the words written in that Book. And Reb Zvi had taken down all that he had said, and Tselya had witnessed all that had transpired. And Hayim Elya saw that a glowing aura surrounded Reb Zvi's face. Then Reb Zvi smiled and said: "Normally, Hayim Elya, you serve as my scribe. But this time it was my honor to serve as yours. Because of you, I too had a glimpse into that Book whose sweetness Ezekiel was permitted to taste. And because of you I have shared in his blessing, for once a blessing has been brought to our people, it can be renewed by those who reach that rung of the ladder. And today, Hayim Elya, you stood on that rung, nor did you fall off. But tell me, please, did you close your eyes because you could not bear to gaze upon such majesty, or because you could not bear to see the Temple torn down?''

And Hayim Elya considered Reb Zvi's question, and he said: "I sensed that had I continued to observe that unveiled splendor, I might have been blinded, and I also felt in danger of cutting the silver cord by which every man's soul is attached. But now I also realize that I am grateful I was spared witnessing the Temple being torn down, for this way it will always remain in my memory as it is in all its glory.''

Then Reb Zvi said: "Just after you shut your eyes, Hayim Elya, and before the scroll was rolled up and taken away, I glanced at it and read there that you had inherited the volume of the *Sefer Raziel* from the side of your grandmother, Rayzel, and not from that of your grandfather. And it was also revealed that your grandmother had been named for that very angel, Raziel, for that is the guardian angel of your family, and that book and parchment have been in your family since the days of the first Temple. Who knows how many times that parchment, folded inside the amulet, protected whoever used it against the dangers of the ascent? But once the amulet had been lost, the parchment was unable to serve its purpose, until you deciphered the meaning of the reference to Ezekiel. This, Hayim Elya, you did by yourself, as must be the case, though Sharya and I took you as close as we could. Now the parchment has fulfilled its purpose, and the Book has been transcribed for another generation.''

THE TALE OF THE KETUBAH

Now the wife of Reb Hayim Elya, whose name was Tselya, which means "the shadow of God," had been born in *Eretz Yisrael*, in the holy city of Jerusalem. For this reason she was regarded by the people of Buczacz as if she were an angelic visitor sent to remind them of the Land they longed for. And for this reason an exception was made for her, and she was permitted to utilize her skill as a *sopher*, a scribe who could write any document except for the Torah and the parchment for the *mezuzah* and *tefillin*. And so it was that she was known especially for the intricate adornment she gave to her *ketubahs*, the contract which established the obligations of the bridegroom to his bride. For among the people it was reasoned that when any vessel was necessary for fulfilling a *mitzvah*, it was proper and fitting to fulfill the *mitzvah* in fine and handsome vessels.

Now one year it happened, on the eve of *Shavuot*, the anniversary of the giving of the Torah at Sinai, that Tselya had a dream in the morning, just before she woke up. In this dream she found herself present at a wedding of supreme importance, where a great many people were in attendance. An old rabbi, of stern appearance and with a long, white beard, was presiding. And he was very solemn and took great care in everything he did. And he announced before the service began that it was an occasion of the utmost significance. If anyone dared to speak out of turn they would be expelled from that place. And everyone was silent. Then Tselya noticed that on each of the four walls of that place there was inscribed a very large *ketubah*. And that *ketubah* had been written in blue on each of the white walls, and the illumination that adorned it was wonderous to behold. And that *ketubah* had been inscribed for the wedding about to take place. And it was then she realized that although the bride and groom were not yet present, the ceremony had begun as if they were; and the wedding took place. Then she woke up.

When Tselya, the wife of Reb Hayim Elya, had awakened, she told this dream to her husband, and Hayim Elya said to himself: "When I see Reb Zvi today I will relate this dream and ask him to tell me what it means." And not long afterwards Hayim Elya came to the home of Reb Zvi. But the moment he stepped into the house, the dream was erased from his memory as if he had never heard it. And when he and Reb Zvi spoke, they spoke of the *Akedah*, the binding of Isaac, even though it was *Erev Shavuot*. And afterwards Hayim Elya went to the *Beit Midrash*, the House of Study. There he found Reb Yakov ben Eliezer in deep contemplation of a text. But as soon as Hayim Elya entered, Reb Yakov got up and came over to him and said: "Today I came across a copy of the *Sephardi Machzor*, which was once left here by a traveller from *Eretz Yisrael*. Finding this book made me remember the traveller who brought it here, and remembering the traveller made me remember *Eretz Yisrael* which, in any case, is never far from my thoughts. And then I decided that I would pray the portion for *Shavuot* from this *Machzor*, and in this way come into greater contact with the Land. Just before you entered I turned to the text of a *ketubah* in this *Machzor* unlike any other I have ever seen. Then Reb Yakov took the book and handed it to Reb Hayim Elya and said: "Here, read this page." And this is what Hayim Elya read there:

> Friday, the sixth of Sivan, the day appointed by the Lord
> for the revelation of the Torah to His beloved people,
> the Invisible One came forth from Sinai. The Bridegroom,
> Ruler of rulers, Prince of princes, said unto the pious and
> virtuous maiden, Israel, who had won His favor above
> all others: "Many days wilt thou be Mine and I will be
> thy Redeemer. Be thou My mate according to the law of
> Moses and Israel, and I will honor, support and maintain
> thee, and be thy shelter and refuge in everlasting mercy.
> And I will set aside for thee the life-giving Torah, by
> which thou and thy children will live in health and tran-
> quility. This Covenant shall be valid and established
> forever and ever." Thus an eternal Covenant, binding
> them forever, has been established between them, and
> the Bridegroom and the bride have given their oaths to
> carry it out. May the Bridegroom rejoice with the bride
> whom He has taken as His lot, and may the bride rejoice
> with the Husband of her youth.

And when Reb Hayim Elya had read this *ketubah*,
which formalized the betrothal of God to His people Israel for all generations, he suddenly understood the meaning of his wife's dream that morning, and why the bride
and groom had not been present at the wedding. And he
understood that the question he had forgotten to ask Reb
Zvi had been answered. Then he hurried to the home of
Reb Zvi, and said: "Rebbe, look at what has happened."
And then he told him the tale, and he said: "But how
is it possible that when I entered your house the dream
was erased from my memory, as if it had never been
there?" And after a long silence Reb Zvi replied:

"It was your destiny, Hayim Elya, to have the secret
of the dream revealed to you in that fashion, as it has
happened, which must surely mean more to you than if
I had simply interpreted the dream. Therefore the dream
was concealed from you until it was time for it to be revealed. But the true meaning of what has occurred is even
much more profound. Know, Hayim Elya, that since
Pesach something has been happening to you. Your mind
has slowly but surely been reaching out to infiltrate and

שׁוֹטֶר בְּאַהֲבָה

become a part of your heart. Gradually your mind has been finding its way, inch by inch, bit by bit. Now, somewhere at your center, the part from which all of your power goes forth—that which you receive from above and impart here below—somewhere at your center a joining is about to take place. Know, Hayim Elya, that your *Zahar*, the powerful masculine center of yourself, and your *Nekevah*, your feminine side, are now attaching back to back. But being back to back each cannot be seen by the other, only felt as the dim presence of a dark shadow. Gradually these two parts must turn to face each other. Know that soon they will be able to see each other through the eyes of wisdom, and that when they face each other then indeed will a marriage take place between them, consummating their union, sanctified by the *ketubah* to be written, by the wisdom that has come to be the witness.''

THE SEPHARDI MACHZOR

for Rabbi Jack Riemer

When the days had ascended near the eve of *Shavuot*, Reb Yakov ben Eliezer remembered the vow he had made to pray on *Shavuot* that year from the *Sephardi Machzor* that had been left in the *Beit Midrash* by the traveller from *Eretz Yisrael*. And the night before the eve of *Shavuot* Reb Yakov had a vivid dream. And in the dream it was already *Shavuot*, and he was dressed in his coat-like *tallis* and praying with his fellow Hasidim who filled the House of Prayer. And then he and the others began to chant a prayer. And although he was certain that he had never before heard that prayer, at the same time he found that he knew its words by heart, and knew the melody equally well. And the words of that prayer were deeply profound and filled with mysteries, and he understood them to the roots of his soul, and the melody haunted him, and he knew it must be Sephardic in origin.

And Reb Yakov ben Eliezer became lost in that melody, and let it lead him upward, like the smoke rising from a burnt offering. And when he reached the top he was

returned to this world like the fire of the Lord that
descends to consume the offering. And then he woke up.
And although he remembered the dream in every detail,
he was unable to recall either the prayer or its melody.
No such prayer was to be found in any book, and he knew
that it did not exist in this world; and now it was gone.

The next evening, when the prayers for *Shavuot* began,
commemorating the Giving of the Torah at Mount Sinai,
Reb Yakov prayed from the *Sephardi Machzor*. And
while he read from that book he was able to recall the
melody he had heard in his dream. Yet when he lifted
his eyes from the page the melody vanished from his
memory, and only the faintest trace of it remained. But
when he brought his eyes back to the page the melody
returned. And still the fact remained that the words of
the prayer were lost, and that he could not recall even
a single word.

And that night Reb Yakov had a dream in which he
sought out his friend Reb Aharon ben Pinhas, for departed
ones may still be sought in the world of dreams. And Reb
Yakov spoke of his intention to pray with the *Sephardi
Machzor* and of the dream that had come of it, and of
the melody that beckoned to him only when his eyes
were fixed on the page. And in the dream Reb Aharon
listened carefully and then he said: "All prayers were first
written on high, Reb Yakov, and if there is need that these
words be said below they are revealed to the poet and
he writes them down. It is in this way that all the true
prayers are composed and come into being. But if there
is no need for these words to be said below, they remain
floating in the high heavens. There the elect of every
generation sense them, as you have, and in this way the
full power of the *tikkun* is brought to repair the Robe
of the *Shekhinah* in the Upper Worlds, and so much
greater is the blessing that comes in turn to us below.

"That such a dream has come to you can only mean
that your soul, Reb Yakov, must have been one of the
six hundred thousand *neshamah*s present at Mount Sinai
at the Giving of the Torah. For at Sinai the Children of
Israel heard every prayer that exists in the Upper Worlds,
even prayers that have not yet been heard again in this

המחזור

הספרדי

world. For everything comes to us from above, and when the time has come for something to be disclosed, then it is sent to one of these souls so that it can be revealed.

"However, there are secrets so hidden that although they must be shared in the Upper Worlds for the *tikkun* to take place, they may not be revealed here below. The prayer that you read in your dream was one of these secrets, Reb Yakov, that is why you remember only the melody when you read the page of that *Machzor*, which reminds you that the secret does exist, even though it must remain hidden in the *Yenne Velt*."

THE LOST PSALM

That Reb Avraham ben Yehoshua was a great scholar and philosopher no one disputed. He had been one of the pillars among men when he had passed away. But among only a few of his generation was it known that he was also a poet. For only one book of his poems and prayers had been published, and that in a private edition, only for his friends. This book was treasured by those who knew it; yet its existence remained obscure, even after his death.

Now it happened in Buczacz that a Hasid who was a printer, and had set with his own hands many of the teachings of the Masters, such as Reb Nachman of Bratslav, decided to publish a book of prayers and great psalms. He drew these from the psalms of David and the prayers of the medieval poets, especially Judah ha-Levi. And he also included prayers of the Hasidim—of the Baal Shem Tov, of Dov Baer, of Levi Yitzhak of Berditchev and, of course, those of Rabbi Nachman.

Now when the printer had completed printing the pages of the book, but had not yet bound them, he showed the galleys to Reb Yakov ben Eliezer, who read them and said: "This book is wonderful, for it is good to find the Fathers of our time standing beside the Fathers of the past. Yet there is one great writer of psalms that you have omitted." Now the printer had combed the sacred literatures carefully for those prayers, and he wondered whom this might be. He asked Reb Yakov about this, and Reb Yakov replied: "You have left out the psalms of Reb Avraham ben Yehoshua!"

The printer was astonished to hear this, and he said: "I did not know that Reb Avraham ben Yehoshua, of blessed memory, was one of those who carried the song of David into our time. But I am afraid it is too late. I have already printed the book, and now I am about to bind it."

Then the printer returned to his home, to begin the work of binding the book. For not only did he print the pages of the books himself, setting them letter by letter, but he also bound them as well. Yet it happened when he returned home that the printer discovered that Reb Zalman of Zholkiev had come to visit him while he was not home. And since he had not been there, Reb Zalman had left him a book. And what book was it? None other than the book of Reb Avraham's poems. And when the printer saw this, he knew that it was a sign that he must not omit Reb Avraham from the book.

Then he sat down and read the text, and he was deeply moved by the poems in which the joys and sorrows of life were evoked, and by the pious prayers he found there. And one of those prayers was entitled "Psalm," and when he read that prayer he knew that he must have it in the book he had just compiled and printed. He picked up the set of the pages of the book, and looked at them, and he discovered that there was a blank page at the very end of the last signature, where that very poem would surely be perfect.

At once the printer arose and began to set the type for that poem, and before long he had set every letter of it, and put it into the printing press. And he printed one copy of it, and saw that it was flawless. Then he took that page and the book and hurried to the home of Reb Yakov ben Eliezer, to show him the miracle of the book.

Now Reb Yakov was surely astonished at this turn of events, but he immediately cautioned the printer that he must first seek permission from Reb Avraham's widow before he included the psalm. The printer, in his excitement, had not thought of this, and although he felt that Reb Avraham's psalm belonged to tradition, and not to any one person, still he realized that he must do as Reb Yakov said. So, with much trepidation, he went to visit the widow of Reb Avraham.

When he arrived the printer showed her the page with Reb Avraham's psalm, and he told her of the book of prayers he had compiled, and asked that he might include that one psalm among them. But when Reb Avraham's widow said no, the world went dark for this printer. He pleaded with the woman, but for reasons of her own, which she would not reveal, she refused. At last the printer departed, his heart broken.

In the days that followed he bound the book, and the page at the end of the last signature he left blank.

When the book was complete, the printer, who was a Hasid of Reb Zvi, showed it to his Rebbe. Then he told Reb Zvi the tale of the psalm that he had been forced to leave out. When he heard the tale Reb Zvi said: "It took great efforts for the spirit of Reb Avraham to inspire Reb Zalman to bring the copy of his book to you on that day, at that time. And when his widow refused you permission, for whatever reason, she obstructed the will of his spirit. But she did not know how strong is that will, much greater than the will of anyone alive."

With that Reb Zvi turned to the last page of the newly bound book. And instead of the blank page that had been there, a poem was inscribed on that page, in a handwriting the printer had seen many times before in his life. It was none other than Reb Avraham's hand, and it was the very psalm that he had selected to include there, on that page.

The printer was speechless when he saw this miracle, but Reb Zvi did not seem surprised. Then Reb Zvi said: "Come, let us go together to the widow of Reb Avraham." This they did, and when they showed her the page, on which was to be found the handwriting of her departed husband, which she knew so well, she broke down in tears, for she understood that she had wronged him. Then she explained why she had refused to permit him to include the poem. It seems that among the poems in that obscure book of Reb Avraham's was one love poem to a woman, long since departed from this world, whom Reb Avraham had loved before he had met and married his wife. For this reason she did not want to draw any attention to the book, and feared that the inclusion of the psalm would cause others to seek it out. Now, however, she saw the ways of her error, and she gave the printer permission to include the poem in all future editions of the book.

And when the first edition of that book was gone, the printer printed and bound another, and the very last poem in that book was none other than the psalm of Reb Avraham of blessed memory.

THE TALE OF THE WEDDING RING

One day it happened that Reb Hayim Elya returned home after praying *Minhah* and *Ma'ariv* and he was met at the door by his wife, Tselya. And Tselya was excited and she said: "When I returned home from the market today I discovered that my gold wedding ring, given to me by your mother, Batya, was missing. I had no idea where I might have dropped it. I was about to retrace my steps when a young woman came to the door, and she said: 'Has anyone here lost a wedding ring?' And I was amazed to see her, and I told her I had despaired of ever finding it again. And she said that her name was Shua, and that she had found it not far from our house. I invited her to come in and she was enchanted by our child, Sharya."

When Hayim Elya heard this—that the wedding ring had become lost and that it had been found in such an unexpected fashion—he decided that he must consult with Reb Zvi about the meaning of this incident. The next morning, after they had prayed *Shahareis*, Hayim Elya told the tale to Reb Zvi, who listened closely. And after Hayim Elya had finished speaking, Reb Zvi said: "The meaning of this episode is clear, Hayim Elya. There exists in your marriage some impediment to spiritual union. This is the union spoken of in the *Zohar*, in which the souls of a man and his wife unite into one soul every evening while they sleep, and ascend Jacob's Ladder into the Heavens and travel through the *Yenne Velt*, the Other World. Now you must return home and bring me three things: the parchment inside your *mezuzah*, the text of the amulet to ward off Lilith that is hung above your child's cradle, and your *ketubah*."

Then Hayim Elya returned home and told his wife about Reb Zvi's request, and they gathered together the *mezuzah*, the amulet, and the *ketubah*, and brought them to Reb Zvi. And Reb Zvi examined each text in great detail, beginning with the parchment inside the *mezuzah*, then the text of the amulet, and then the *ketubah*. And after he had studied them for a very long time, he concluded that every letter and every crown was in its place, and this puzzled him. But what was even more puzzling was the fact that while the texts of the *mezuzah* and the amulet were written on parchment, the *ketubah* of Hayim Elya and his wife was only written on paper. And Reb Zvi asked them why this was, and it was Tselya who replied, and she said: "You should know, Rebbe, that since I am a *sopher* it has been my intention to make my own *ketubah* on a piece of parchment that I have been saving for this purpose. For the *ketubah* in your hands, written on paper, was only intended to be temporary, until I could find time to make one of my own."

And Reb Zvi said: "Now I understand! But let us go back to the beginning, to the loss of your wedding ring. That, Tselya, meant that you had attracted the attention of the Evil Eye. But the fact that the ring was returned in such miraculous fashion demonstrates quite strongly that your marriage is in no danger, and that the powers of *tikkun*, of Restoration and Redemption, are very great in your lives. Therefore I expected to find the imperfection in one of the letters in one of these texts. But now I understand that the imperfection is due to the fact that the true contract, the one that will make your marriage eternally valid and binding, has yet to be written. Hurry,

Tselya, waste no more time. You must complete the *ketubah* before the first of *Kislev*."

Now the first of *Kislev* fell in five days, and the normal time for Tselya to inscribe a *ketubah* and complete it with all her many beautiful flourishes was seven days. And so it was that Tselya worked on this *ketubah* as if she were in a trance, and lived as if in a vision. And while she worked on it the child was fragile and Hayim Elya felt that his spirit was exhausted, and everything hung in the balance. And she lived in that trance for four days, and at the end of the fourth day the *ketubah* was complete. And it had been drawn in the shape of a circle, so that their marriage would be like the full moon in Jerusalem on the night of their wedding. And inscribed inside that circle it read: "Forty days before they were born it was revealed that these two, whose souls are like twin stars, shall meet and be married in Jerusalem, the city that is itself a bride." And she used an ink that made the letters look like flames on the parchment. And she surrounded the text with gold leaf and intricate designs. And beneath the text of the *ketubah* she wrote in gold letters: *"V'hakol Sharir V'kayam,"* "It is valid and binding."

And the days that followed the completion of the *ketubah* were a time of abundance in the lives of Hayim Elya and Tselya and their child. For the new time had arrived, and with it good fortune. Just as the sun shines forth in redoubled beauty after a rain, so the new era appeared all the more glorious in contrast to the old.

THE WOMAN IN THE CAVE

One night, not long after she was married, Tselya, the wife of Reb Hayim Elya, had a strange and vivid dream. In the dream she was walking down the aisle of the synagogue when all at once the aisle turned into a path, which soon led her to a dark cave. At first she was afraid, and was about to turn back, when she heard a voice calling out to her from the cave. Then she overcame her fear and entered the cave, where she found steps leading downward. She descended to the bottom of those steps, and there, shining out of the darkness, she saw the face of an old woman.

In the dream Tselya tried to discern the rest of the woman's body, but she could not. It was hidden in the darkness. Tselya thought to herself that the woman must be wearing a long, black gown, for how else could she disappear so completely into the dark? But the old woman's face was vivid in every respect, and her eyes were fixed on Tselya, who stood before her in awe. For even though she was old, her face was very beautiful, and her hair, which was braided, reached down to her back. Then the old woman broke the silence and said:

"Where is Hayim Elya? Why is it that you have come here instead of him? It was he that I summoned."

Now Tselya was greatly confused when she heard this, for she had assumed that the old woman had called for her to come there. But before Tselya could reply, the old woman spoke again, and said: "Go back where you came from, and bring Hayim Elya here at once. But this time only he must descend into the cave." And when this command had been made, Tselya felt that she had no choice but to obey it, and she climbed up the stone steps and departed from the cave at once. She followed the path that had led her there until it turned into the aisle of the synagogue, and there she found Hayim Elya, reading the pages of a sacred text.

She hurried to him and told him what had happened, how he had been summoned by the old woman. Then Hayim Elya did not hesitate, but joined Tselya at once, and they followed the aisle once more until it became the path that led them both to the cave. But when they reached the entrance of the cave, Tselya did not tell Hayim Elya that he was to descend there alone. For she wondered greatly at the identity of the old woman and what it was that she was going to say. Therefore she descended with him, and when they reached the bottom step, the face of the old woman hovered in the darkness before them, and this time she seemed angry. She said: "I told you that Hayim Elya must descend alone into this place. Because you have disobeyed me, I cannot reveal to Hayim Elya the reason he was summoned here."

Then, greatly disappointed, Tselya and Hayim Elya turned around and climbed up the stone steps, and just as they reached the last step and were about to step into the light, Tselya awoke, with the dream vividly imprinted on her memory. She found herself beside Hayim Elya, who happened to wake up at the same time. Then Tselya knew that she must tell him the dream, and so she did, in every respect. And Hayim Elya was so astonished by it that the first thing he did was to write it down, so that no detail should be forgotten.

Then Hayim Elya dressed at once, and left the house within a short time, even though the sun had not yet risen. For he knew that such a dream bore with it an important message, although he could not discern what this message might be.

Without even thinking about it, Hayim Elya found himself hurrying toward the synagogue, where Tselya had first been led to the mysterious old woman. But the familiar path to the synagogue did not lead him there, as it always had, but led him instead into a forest. And when he had gone as far as he would have gone to reach the synagogue, he came upon a cave, one he had never seen before. And he knew at once that this must be the cave of which Tselya had dreamed. And as he realized this, a chill ran down his spine, and he wondered if he dared to enter that cave.

Just as Hayim Elya reached the mouth of the cave, he heard his name called out. Then he knew that he could not turn back, and he entered the darkness and slowly made his way down stone steps, feeling his way. He counted the steps, one by one, as he descended, and when he had counted ten steps he reached the cool floor of the cave, completely swathed in darkness except for the shining face of the old woman. And even though he had never seen her before, still he recognized her, and knew that she was the very woman Tselya had encountered in her dream. And all at once Hayim Elya grew very calm, and knew that he was destined to be there. And he became quiet and receptive, waiting to learn what it was that the old woman had summoned him to reveal.

Then the old woman spoke and said: "Countless generations ago a request was made by your ancestor, Abraham, the distinguished patriarch of your ancient family. Now, at last, the request is to be fulfilled." Here the old woman paused, while Hayim Elya considered what she had said. At last he spoke up, hoping that she would tell him more. He said: "What was the request that was made?" And the old woman said: "An audience was requested with the king. Now it is to take place. Follow me."

With that the head of the old woman turned, and Hayim Elya hurried after her, although he could barely make out her shape in the darkness. She led him down endless passages in that dark cave. At last he saw a golden glow arising in the distance, and as he approached this glow it assumed the shape of a huge, golden door. Already the old woman had disappeared in the darkness of the branching maze. Approaching the golden door, Hayim Elya knocked softly and waited. There was no reply. He knocked louder and louder, but still no answer came. At last the desire to know what lay beyond that door became so intense it almost overwhelmed him, and he knew that he would not rest until he learned what lay there. Then, all at once, the floor on which he stood, the ceiling and the golden door melted, merging for a minute of death into the memory of an infant sun, tail of a comet, breath drawn back and forth through countless stars. Around him vessels split open, scattering sparks of light, and much later the same sparks were gathered together and the vessels restored. And when the passage reappeared, he saw melting gold running down the walls, collecting on a pool on the floor, out of which leaped the old woman who had guided him to that place. She was speaking to him, but since he had not heard, she repeated herself: the audience was ended.

At that very moment Hayim Elya awoke, and much to his amazement he found himself at home, lying upon his bed with Tselya, his wife, asleep beside him. And that is when he remembered the dream she had told him in the middle of the night. But he had not arisen as he had believed, but rather fallen back to sleep. And all that he had experienced after that was also a dream. And when he recalled the dream, which had been so real while it had been happening, Hayim Elya was overwhelmed. For then he understood that the dream had been meant for him, but somehow Tselya had received it. And when she had understood this, she had shared it with him, making it possible for him to meet with the old woman after all. And now that it was over, Hayim Elya saw the world bathed in a new light, that of the Holy One, blessed be He, and knew that the long-awaited audience had indeed taken place.

THE TALE OF THE GIFT

Once Reb Reuven Avraham ben Hershel, chief scribe of the *Kehillah*, the community of Buczacz, came to Tselya, wife of Reb Hayim Elya, and asked her to write a new *ketubah* that he might give to his wife Bracha for their tenth anniversary. This Tselya undertook to do, and no sooner did she touch her pen to the parchment than the letters began to fly over the page. And Tselya understood what this meant. For she had come to recognize that sometimes a *ketubah* would almost write itself, while at other times the pen would resist each and every word. And what signs were these? Tselya had concluded that in those cases in which the Covenant had already been signed above, it was almost effortless to copy it here below. But if a *bat kol*, a heavenly voice, had not gone forth forty days before the birth of each of the betrothed, then the pen was reluctant to confirm the contract. So it was that when she finished that *ketubah* in one day, which had never before happened, Tselya understood that it was meant to come into being.

That same night Reb Reuven Avraham came to Tselya's home with his wife, and there, with Reb Hayim Elya and

Tselya as witnesses, he presented his wife with the new *ketubah*. And Bracha was greatly delighted with this gift, and it was precious in her sight. A few days later Tselya met Bracha in the market, and she took Tselya aside and told her a dream she had had that day. In the dream she had prayed that she and her husband would stay together at least another year—for that is all the blessing we may request, since our covenant with the Holy One is renewed each year and signed in the Book of Life. After this Bracha looked up in the dream and noticed that one wall in her house was empty, and she remembered the *ketubah* she had just received from her husband, and she picked it up to hang in that empty place. And as she touched its wooden frame she heard a voice say: "Your prayer has been granted. But not only for one year, but for ten."

When Tselya reported this dream to Reb Hayim Elya, he knew at once that it should be brought to Reb Zvi's attention, for surely there was a secret concealed in it. And Reb Zvi listened to the tale, nodding his head, so that it almost seemed as if he had heard it before. Then he said: "This is very good news, Hayim Elya. It seems as if the *ketubah* Tselya wrote for this couple will truly serve them well. That must mean that Tselya is able to receive the power of the letters and the words and to transmit it so that they can fulfill their blessings.

"So too does Reb Reuven Avraham, who went to Tselya in the first place to have the new ketubah written, show great insight into the need to renew. For not only a *ketubah* must be renewed once in every cycle, which lasts ten years, but even the Torah must be given again. So it is that each year on *Yom Kippur* it is not only our individual fate that hangs in the balance, but the right of our nation to continue to possess—no, to receive anew—the scroll which serves as the pillar that supports the world. For is it not possible that if we prove unworthy of receiving it, that one year the fruit will not take form, the harvest will not take place, and the gift which each year must be given again will be refused or given to another nation? Since it is the seed which determines the fruit, in undertaking this act of *teshuvah*, of turning back and beginning again, Reb Reuven Avraham has planted

בלב ראשון בשבת
אחד עשר יום לחדש שבט
שנת חמשת אלפים ושבע מאות עשרים ושבע
למנין שאנו מנין כאן סאנטו לואיס במדינת אמריקי הצפונית
איך החתן ראובן אברהם בן הירצל למשפחת בדן אמר
להדא בתולתא בירכה בת יעקב למשפחת לוי הוי
לי לאנתו כדת משה וישראל ואנא אפלח ואוקיר ואיזון ואפרנס
יתכי ליכי כהלכות גוברין יהודאין דפלחין ומוקרין וזנין ומפרנסין
לנשיהון בקושטא ויהיבנא ליכי מהר בתוליכי כסף זוזי מאתן דחזי
ליכי מדאורייתא ומזוניכי וכסותיכי וסיפוקיכי ומיעל לותיכי כאורח כל
ארעא וצביאת מרת בירכה בתולתא דא והות ליה לאנתו ודן נדוניא דהנעלת
ליה מבי אבוה בין בכסף בין בדהב בין בתכשיטין במאני דלבושא בשמושי דירה
ובשמושא דערסא הכל קבל עליו ראובן אברהם חתן דנן במאה זקוקים כסף צרוף וצבי
ראובן אברהם חתן דנן והוסיף לה מן דיליה עוד מאה זקוקים כסף צרוף אחרים כנגדן
סך הכל מאתים זקוקים כסף צרוף וכן אמר ראובן אברהם חתן דנן אחריות שטר כתובתא דא
ודוניא דן ותוספתא דא קבלית עלי ועל ירתי בתראי להתפרע מכל שפר ארג נכסין וקנינין
דאית להון אחריות ודלית להון אחרית בכלהון יהון אחראין וערבאין לפרוע מנהון שטר כתובתא
דא ודוניא דן ותוספתא דא אפלו מן אפלו מאן גלימא דעל כתפאי בחיי ובתר חיי מן יומא דנן
ולעלם ואחריות שטר כתובתא דא ודוניא דן ותוספתא דא קבל עליו ראובן אברהם חתן דנן
כחומר כל שטרי כתובות ותוספתות דנהגין בבת ישראל העשוין כתקון חכמינו זכרונם
לברכה דלא כאסמכתא ודלא כטופסי דשטרי וקנינא מן ראובן אברהם חתן דנל
למשפחת בדן חתן דנן למרת בירכה בת יעקב למשפחת לוי בתולתא דא
על כל מה דכתוב ומפורש לעיל במנא דכשר למקנא ביה הכל שריר וקים

_____ עד _____ לאום רב חיים אשי ד _____ על ____ לאום ____ ד'יה _____ עד

the seed that will surely bear the fruit of *tikkun*, of restoration.

"But most of all the credit for this restoration rests with Bracha. For it was she who heard the *bat kol*, the voice that went forth, and it was she whose prayer the Holy One granted!"

A SIGN FROM ON HIGH

One day while Tselya, the wife of Reb Hayim Elya, was visiting with an old friend from *Eretz Yisrael*, a letter was delivered from the woman's daughter, who lived in the nearby town of Kotzk. In the letter her daughter, who was shortly expecting to give birth, wrote her mother of her fear that she might lose the child, for there had been signs of blood. Naturally her mother was very distraught, and she began to sob.

Now it happened that while the woman was opening the letter, Tselya, who had been standing by the library in that home, reached out and selected a book at random and pulled it out. When she did, something fell from it, and when Tselya picked it up she saw that it was an amulet against Lilith, one of whose faces is that of the child-destroying witch. And when her friend read her the letter from her daughter, Tselya wondered if there might be a link between the letter and the amulet she had found at the same time.

That night Tselya told Reb Hayim Elya of this odd occurrence, and the next day Hayim Elya reported it to Reb Zvi. And Reb Zvi said: "Surely her finding the amulet at

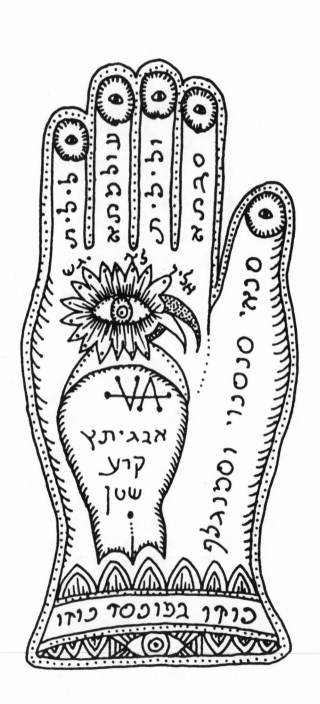

that very moment was a sign from on high. Go this very instant, Hayim Elya, and see to it that the amulet your wife found there is delivered to this young woman as soon as possible. For she desperately requires its protection!''

Hayim Elya did not doubt for an instant that Reb Zvi was correct in this, and he rushed out of the house and returned home, where he reported the Rebbe's words to his wife. And she, in turn, hurried to the home of her friend, and together they went from door to door until they found a messenger to deliver the amulet to her daughter that very day.

Less than a month later news reached Buczacz that this young woman had given birth to a fine and healthy child, and all gave thanks to the Holy One, blessed be He, for protecting that child in its hour of danger.

THE TALE OF THE RESCUED TORAHS

It happened one year that the ship in which Reb Reuven Avraham ben Hershel returned from a pilgrimage to the Holy Land was caught in a storm, during which the ship was damaged and thrown off course. In this way the pilgrims reached the port of Tangiers in the land of Morocco. There they learned that their voyage would be delayed for several weeks while the ship was repaired. At first they were distressed, but it was then that Reb Reuven Avraham recalled that Maimonides, of blessed memory, had made his home for many years in the ancient city of Fez, also in Morocco, and at his suggestion the pilgrims agreed to pay a visit to the home of Maimonides in that city.

Upon their arrival in Fez the pilgrims had the good fortune to be greeted by a tall, serene old Jew, erect despite his advanced years, wearing a maroon Fez cap on his head. And the name of that old man—the Patriarch of the Sephardic community of Fez and one of the last Jewish residents—was Reb Yakov ben Shimon. Reb Yakov was overjoyed to meet the pilgrims, especially since they had just returned from the Holy Land, and he put himself at their service. Together they went to the ancient home of Maimonides, where the pilgrims saw the thirteen protrusions of the building and heard the thirteen chimes of the clock, each protrusion and chime representing one of the Thirteen Principles of Maimonides.

For the next week the pilgrims were honored by the ancient memories of Reb Yakov, who recalled the history of the Jews of that community from the time of Maimonides until then. In recent years, due to the oppressions they had endured, the community of Fez had been reduced to a handful of old people who had chosen to remain.

Now the pilgrims were fascinated by these tales of Reb Yakov, and became caught up in the history of that ill-fated community. Thus it happened that they asked Reb Yakov to take them to the synagogue of Fez, now abandoned. And then, for the first time, the old man became emotional and rose and left the room, causing the pilgrims to fear that they had touched on a subject too painful to bear. But in a short time Reb Yakov returned, and in his possession, wrapped in yellowed parchment, were the keys to the synagogue building. He told the pilgrims that he had last tried to enter the Sallah synagogue six years before, only to have the keys fail to work.

Then seven of the pilgrims, including Reb Reuven Avraham, followed the old man through a confusing maze of streets of the old medina, which were joined together by darkly forboding alleyways. The smells of incense and hashish filled the air, and the natives of Fez gave them curious and sometimes threatening stares. It had been raining, and the cobblestones were slippery, and before long the pilgrims were tired and hungry and felt faint from the strangeness of the place.

On and on they walked, trailing the determined old man who carried the keys that had already unlocked many memories. So far did he lead them that the pilgrims began to fear that he might have forgotten the way.

Finally they followed him into an especially dark alleyway filled with Arab street urchins, whose curiosity became aroused by the strange group. All stared as the old man fumbled along a greenish wall with his key. At

last a door creaked open, and the dim light revealed a stairway which spiraled sharply to the left. On entering, the faces of the pilgrims were caught in cobwebs which hung from the floor to the ceiling. They expected to find the building gutted, but instead the pilgrims found themselves in the presence of a magnificent synagogue. Intricate, filigreed carvings and blue and white tilework graced the walls and supporting pillars. Although everything was covered with inches of dust, it looked as if it had been abandoned in the middle of a service. Prayer books were open on wooden benches; *kippot* and *tallisim* lay beneath the dust, as did an elegantly upholstered ritual chair. Valuable but tarnished silver ornaments, on which *Yahrzeit* candles had been suspended, hung from the ceiling.

As the pilgrims stared at the unexpected beauty of that abandoned holy place, they did not notice that the street urchins had followed them inside, their eyes taking in the interior. Now one of the urchins spotted a rusted *tzedakah* box on one of the benches and sought to grab it. Just then one of the pilgrims let out a yell, and the urchins fled from that place. Then, when the pilgrims turned back to the debris on the floor, and the dust, the images of a once proud community struck them with their full force, and many began to sob.

Then the old man approached the Holy Ark and parted the doors and all gasped. To the surprise of even the old man, three magnificent Torah scrolls rested in the ark. The sight was too much for the old man, as well as for the others. He started to weep, and between sobs he told the pilgrims that the scrolls would not be safe from theft if left in the ark, since the street urchins now knew about that place. They had to be moved. The law required that Torahs must be protected.

And so the seven pilgrims, forming an unlikely caravan, took turns carrying the Torah scrolls up the winding streets. They walked into the cool darkness of the alley and past the urchins, who stood watching wide-eyed. Once in the sunlight they were stared at by all who saw them, and some of the remarks were hostile. After what seemed an eternity, they found their way back to the main street, and at last they reached the inn where they were staying. The Torahs had been saved, and it was then that they heard the news that the ship had been restored and was ready to sail. The Torahs were entrusted to the safekeeping of Reb Yakov, and with many fond farewells the pilgrims took their leave for Tangiers and the waiting ship.

THE TALE OF LILITH

Now it happened that there lived in the city of Buczacz a woman who practiced witchcraft. And this woman had made an unholy alliance with the demoness Lilith, once the first wife of Adam, before Eve. Lilith had tired of the Garden of Eden and of Adam and had abandoned him one day by pronouncing the secret Name of God and flying out of the Garden to a cave beside the Red Sea, where she took for her lovers all the demons who made their home there. When the Holy One sent three angels to order her to return to her husband, this harlot had refused, and as a punishment one hundred of her demon offspring were condemned to die every day.

In revenge Lilith became a child-destroying witch, seeking to harm human children, and she can only be warded off if the pregnant woman wears an amulet. And the amulet is only effective because the three angels forced Lilith to vow to respect the command of its incantation. In this way a pregnant woman can be protected, and once the child is born the amulet can be hung above the cradle to keep Lilith away. Inside the amulet there is a parchment on which the words "Out, Lilith!" have been written in large letters, and beneath them is the following inscription:

> I adjure you, Lilith, in the Name of the Holy One, Blessed be He, and in the names of the three angels sent after you, Senoy, Sansenoy and Semangelof, to remember the vow you made that wherever you find their names you will cause no harm, neither you nor your cohorts; and in their names and in the names of the seals set down here, I adjure you, Queen of Demons, and all your multitudes, to cause no harm to a woman while she carries a child nor when she gives birth, nor to the children born to her, neither during the day nor during the night, neither through their food nor through their drink, neither in their head nor in their hearts. By the strength of these names and seals I so adjure you, Lilith, and all your offspring, to obey this command.

Further, it is known that Lilith's lust is so great that she seeks to crawl beneath the sheets of men who sleep in a house alone and seduce them into having intercourse with her, and the offspring of this union are all the demons that populate the world. That is why a man must recite Psalm 91 at the funeral of his father in order to protect himself from these demon offspring, who would otherwise try to steal his inheritance.

Now this woman who had allied herself with Lilith was deeply jealous of Reb Hayim Elya and his wife Tselya, for they had a fine girl-child whose name was Sharya, which means "God sang". And this witch was childless, for she had married an old man, who was far past the age of child-bearing even when they stood beneath the *Huppah*. And this woman was also jealous of the love between Hayim Elya and his wife, for her own marriage was loveless. For these reasons she was filled with hatred.

Then it happened that Reb Hayim Elya had a dream in the middle of one night, a dream that was vivid and disturbing. In this dream he became aware of the presence of this witch and her husband at his door. And in the dream he understood that though it looked like this woman, it was actually Lilith whom this woman had sent to harm his family. Nor was it actually her husband who had acompanied her, but Asmodeus, Prince of Demons,

למזל טוב

שיר המעלות

אֶשָּׂא עֵינַי אֶל - הֶהָרִים
מֵאַיִן יָבוֹא עֶזְרִי ; עֶזְרִי מֵעִם ה' עֹשֵׂה שָׁמַיִם וָאָרֶץ
אַל - יִתֵּן לַמּוֹט רַגְלֶךָ אַל - יָנוּם שֹׁמְרֶךָ ; הִנֵּה לֹא - יָנוּם
וְלֹא יִישָׁן שׁוֹמֵר יִשְׂרָאֵל ; ה' שֹׁמְרֶךָ ה' צִלְּךָ עַל - יַד יְמִינֶךָ
יוֹמָם הַשֶּׁמֶשׁ לֹא - יַכֶּכָּה וְיָרֵחַ בַּלָּיְלָה ; ה' יִשְׁמָרְךָ מִכָּל
רָע יִשְׁמֹר אֶת - נַפְשֶׁךָ ; ה' יִשְׁמָר - צֵאתְךָ וּבוֹאֶךָ מֵעַתָּה
וְעַד - עוֹלָם :

שדי	קרע	שטן
סיע	יסנסים	וסמנגלוף

מכשפה לא תחיה	פנימה	תחיה לא כשפה
לא תחיה מכשפה	אדם וחוה	לא כשפה תחיה
מכשפה תחיה לא	אברהם ושרה	מכשפה תחיה לא
	יצחק ורבקה	
לילית וכל כת	יעקב לאה ורחל	חילה חוצה
בשם ה' אלהי ישראל		ימין רפאל

ומשמאלי גבריאל כלפני אוריאל ומאחורי רפאל ועל ראשי שכינת - אל

who travels with Lilith on her nightly journeys. And they did not knock on the door, but opened it and entered. And Hayim Elya did not hesitate when this happened, but rose up from his bed and approached them and said: "Get out! You are not welcome in this house!" Then, with reluctance and with hate in their eyes they turned around and slowly walked out. And this time when Hayim Elya closed the door he locked it. And outside the door he heard the two of them making obscene comments to each other that were intended to taunt him. And Hayim Elya lay back on his bed, but he did not sleep.

And before long Lilith crept back into the house. This time she did not open the door, but slipped under it like a shadow, a shadow that Hayim Elya saw flit along the walls. And in a flash Hayim Elya leapt from his bed and screamed at Lilith, whose shadow hovered above his child's bed: "Out, Lilith!" And this time the demoness did not hesitate at all, but vanished in a flash, her shadow scurrying across the walls and beneath the door. Then Hayim Elya understood that this ancient incantation still held power over Lilith, and that she must obey its command. And then he woke up.

At the very moment he opened his eyes, Hayim Elya heard his wife Tselya say to him: "What is it that you said? Your mouth formed words and you seemed very agitated, but the words did not form themselves into sounds." But Hayim Elya did not want to tell his wife the dream, for he was afraid it would frighten her. He realized for the first time how great was the hatred of this witch, and he recognized the danger; nor did he forget that the craven demoness liked to mete out revenge on helpless infants. And Hayim Elya did not reply to her question, but said: "Bring in the baby, and let her spend the rest of the night with us." And Tselya did not ask why, but brought the child into the bedroom, and Hayim Elya put his arms around his child and held her, and did not sleep.

Then it happened that about two hours later Tselya awoke with a start. And she turned to Hayim Elya, who was still awake, and said: "I just had a terrible dream. I dreamed that there was a knock at the door and when

I went to answer it there was a young girl standing there dressed in black. I asked her what she wanted and she said she wanted to come in. And I asked you, and you took one look at her and said: 'Don't let her step inside!' So I closed the door, and from the inside I heard her climb the stairs to the home of our neighbors, who have no children. And she did not knock at their door, but waited in the dark, and after a short time she crept back down the stairs, ever so quietly, and she had a key of her own and she opened the door and came inside. And in less than a minute she emptied out the house, and took everything."

When Hayim Elya heard this dream a chill ran down his body, for he knew that Lilith was indeed present there at that very moment. And he sat up and peered into the darkness and got out of bed and took down the amulet from above the cradle, and he held out the amulet before him and shouted with all his might: "Out, Lilith!" And just then a strong wind blew the door open and a fresh breeze blew in and the air in the house was pure again, and the moon, that had been eclipsed all night by dark clouds, emerged.

THE TALE OF THE SOPHER

for Rabbi James S. Diamond

One night in the month of *Shavat*, Reb Hayim Elya dreamed that he and Reb Yosef ben Mayer were journeying together to the mountain where the Baal Shem had once sealed in stone the Book of Mysteries given to him by Rabbi Adam. And why were they travelling to that place? Because Reb Hayim Elya knew the secret of where the Book had been hidden, but he did not know how to pronounce the Name that was the only key to unlock that stone. And Reb Yosef had come with him although he did not know where the Book had been hidden, because he did know how to pronounce the Name. Together those two secrets could unseal the Book.

In the dream they travelled a great distance to that mountain, overcoming many obstacles. Then they struggled to climb the mountain itself, and at last Hayim Elya pointed to the place where the Book had been sealed. Instinctively, they knew they must unseal the Book before dawn; and only a short span of time remained before the first wings of light would appear. Suddenly Reb Yosef looked down from that high place and was distracted, torn like a page from a book, and unable to pronounce the Name. Nor could he reveal it to Hayim Elya, to pronounce instead. For the secret of the Name had flown from his possession, as if it had taken wing in that place. And as the dream ended the sky began to grow light, and the Book remained sealed in the stone.

When Hayim Elya awoke from this dream and recalled it, he was gripped with fury, and his anger at Reb Yosef knew no bounds, for the opportunity to unseal the Book had been lost.

Then Hayim Elya went to see Reb Zvi, and told him his dream. And no sooner had Reb Zvi heard this dream than he stood up and said: "Hurry, Hayim Elya, waste no time. Go to Reb Yosef at once."

Then Hayim Elya hurried so that he might reach the *Beit Midrash*, the House of Study, where Reb Yosef could be found. And when Reb Yosef saw Hayim Elya he said: "Hayim Elya! It is good that you have come. For last night I had a dream in which we travelled together, but since waking it has flown from my grasp."

And Hayim Elya was dumbstruck when he heard this, for then he knew that the dream must have been true, and that the chance to unseal the Book of Mysteries had truly been lost. He told the dream to Reb Yosef, whose dream was then restored to his memory, for the two dreams had been identical in every respect.

Suddenly Hayim Elya's anger returned twofold, and he said: "But why did you hold back the pronunciation of the Name at the last minute? The world thirsts for the secrets contained in that Book. Now they remain sealed, and who knows for how long?"

Just then the door of that *Beit Midrash* opened, and a man entered there whom Hayim Elya had never met. And Reb Yosef was relieved not to have to reply to Hayim Elya's question. Instead he introduced Hayim Elya to the stranger, who turned out to be a *sopher*, a writer of Torahs and sacred documents. He had just arrived in Buczacz from Warsaw, since there were no *sophers* in Buczacz, except for Tselya, wife of Hayim Elya, who was not permitted to do the writing or repairing of a Torah

scroll, or a *mezuzah* or *tefillin*, because she was a woman. And why had that *sopher* come to that *Beit Midrash*? To repair one of the Torahs in the *Beit Knesset*, the House of Prayer, adjacent to that House of Study. And what was wrong with the Torah that it needed repair? Through long use it had torn in two places, and several words were in need of restoration.

And then Hayim Elya realized that this *sopher* from a distant city had entered that place to perform an act of *tikkun*, of restoration. For it is said that he who restores the Torah also repairs the robe of the *Shekhinah*, the Divine Presence, who hovers above the parchment of the scroll like a flame casting its illumination. Then Hayim Elya recognized that the arrival of the *sopher* was no accident, but an omen. And he realized that in this way the Holy One had sent them a message that they should not sever their ties, any more than they would tear out a *parashah* of the Torah. And just as the *sopher* had come to perform the *tikkun* of restoring the Torah, so was it a sign that such a *tikkun* should also take place between Reb Yosef and himself.

Hayim Elya grew calm. All the rancor he had felt for Reb Yosef was gone. Still, he was curious to know what Reb Yosef would say in reply to his question. And when the *sopher* departed to begin the work of restoration, Reb Yosef turned to Hayim Elya and said: "Why did I refuse to pronounce the Name in that place? Because at that moment I looked down into the depths of the Abyss, and I felt like an intruder in that place. And then it was too late—the Name vanished from my lips and from my memory, not as if it had been forgotten, but as if it had never been revealed to me in the first place. How could I have told you this at that time? Therefore I was silent."

When Hayim Elya heard this explanation, he understood that it had been their destiny to reach that far, but no further, and that a barrier had been raised before them, not unlike the gate before the Garden of Eden, that is guarded by an angel with a flaming sword, who bars the way to the Tree of Life. Yet he still had not lost his longing to read in that Book of Mysteries.

Later Hayim Elya returned to Reb Zvi and reported all

that had taken place. And when he had heard this tale, Reb Zvi had this to say: "If only that *sopher* had been your companion on the quest, you would have unsealed the stone. For surely he also knew the secret of the Name, nor would he have looked down at the last minute, but kept his attention fixed on that Word as he does on every letter and crown of the Torah that is in need of restoration."

THE ANCIENT SCRIBE

for Tom and Laya Seghi

Among the rebbes of Buczacz, the oldest and most admired were Reb Zvi ben Mordecai and his younger brother, Reb Avraham. Reb Zvi was acknowledged by all as the supreme scholar of the Talmud in Buczacz, and Reb Avraham was the town *mohel*. Each brother had his own Hasidim, who were loyal to them in every respect.

One day Reb Avraham called in one of his youngest Hasidim, Reb Moshe, and said: "Moshe, I have a mission for you of the utmost importance. I have been waiting for the one Hasid right to undertake it, and now I see that it is you. For there is a book that must be recovered, the only existing copy of an ancient text, *Sefer Kelim*. And it has been revealed to me in a dream that your *mazel*, combined with that of your wife, might be sufficient to overcome the forces of evil and restore the lost book.

Now Reb Moshe had heard of the *Sefer Kelim*, but he had believed it to be completely lost, like the *Sefer Raziel*, which God had first revealed to Adam. Then it did not

take him long to agree to this quest, for above all Reb
Moshe wished to restore that which had been lost. Then
Reb Avraham sent him first to the city of Bratslav, where
Reb Nachman had once made his home. For the dream
had revealed to the rebbe that Reb Moshe should begin
there. And once he was there Reb Moshe was to seek out
an old man, one who knew of all the old generations.

When Reb Moshe and his wife, Leah, reached Bratslav, they asked to know where such a man could be
found. So it was that they were directed to the old
shammes of the *Beit Midrash* that had once been used
by Reb Nachman, for the *shammes* also served as the
keeper of the texts. The old man did indeed recall that
copy of *Sefer Kelim*, which he had seen in his youth. He
even recalled the name of the scribe who had written the
copy. And when Reb Moshe learned the name of the
scribe, he was filled with hope, for perhaps the book had
been kept in the scribe's family. But the old *shammes* did
not know from what city the scribe had come. Only that
there was in that library another manuscript written by
that same scribe. This he took out and showed him, and
Reb Moshe studied the way in which each letter had been
formed until it was imprinted in his memory, so that he
would be certain to recognize the work of that same
scribe should he encounter another manuscript copied
in the same hand.

Later that day Reb Moshe's wife, Leah, went to the
Mikvah in that town with the wife of the *shammes*, for
it was the time to do so. There in the *Mikvah* she met
a very old, nearly ancient, woman. No less than ninety
years old and childless, yet she still bled each month like
a young woman. And when Leah spoke with her she
learned that the old woman's name was Sarah, and that
she still hoped for a child to be born. After she had
spoken, Leah told her why she and Reb Moshe had come
to that town. So too did Leah tell her the name of the
scribe whose descendants they were seeking.

Then this Sarah told her that she recognized the name,
and that the last she had heard the descendents of that
scribe lived in the city of Uman, where there had been
a terrible pogrom in the 17th century. The old woman

did not know if any of these descendents were still alive, since she had met one of them only in her youth. But this news was enough to fill Leah with joy, and she thanked the old woman and hurried back to Reb Moshe to tell him what she had learned.

The next day she and Reb Moshe set out for Uman, reaching it seven days later. Those days were exceptionally beautiful, the air was clear and not too cold, and above them came the endless sound of the beating of wings. Flocks of geese flew above, following that same path, for it was November and they were heading for the south of Poland.

When the couple arrived in Uman they asked the whereabouts of the family of that old scribe. They were soon directed to an old house on the outskirts of town, and there they met an old man. They told him the reason they had sought him out, and he told them that his great grandfather was indeed the scribe who had made the last copy of that ancient text. And Reb Moshe and his wife were astounded when the old man told them that his great-grandfather was still alive, although on his deathbed.

Then the old man led them to the room of his great grandfather. Although he was old and shriveled up like an orange peel in the sun, the eyes of the old man still burned clearly. He listened carefully when told of the text they had come so far to seek out. And the old scribe pointed towards one wall of his library, which filled that room. Then the old man who was the scribe's great-grandson searched there, and soon pulled out a single text, which was none other than the very manuscript they sought, the long-lost *Sefer Kelim*.

And when the old scribe saw that they had found it, and how precious it was in their eyes, he smiled a pure and wonderful smile and departed from this world. And when they saw that smile, all were certain that he had remained living until that moment, to know that the last copy of the book would reach those for whom it was intended.

And when Reb Moshe opened the manuscript, he saw written on the first page the names of all those who had received it. The first name written there was that of the old scribe, and after that followed the names of all his children, and their children, until the generation of the old man who was his great grandson. And the last names written there were none other than that of Reb Avraham ben Mordecai, who had sent them on that quest, and that of Reb Moshe himself. And when Reb Moshe saw his name inscribed there, in the hand of the newly departed scribe, he gasped and almost fainted. And from that moment on his faith in the power of the Holy One was never shaken for as long as a single moment.

Later, when Reb Moshe at last delivered the last copy of the *Sefer Kelim* to Reb Avraham, the Rebbe wept tears of joy to hold it in his hands. But when Reb Moshe showed him his own name inscribed there, in the very pen of the ancient scribe, who had kept himself alive until it had reached his hands, Reb Avraham was filled with awe. And after that he studied that book every day, and he held its truths close to his heart. And his Hasidim learned from his lips the truths that had been concealed there so long. But especially did he direct his teachings toward Reb Moshe, whose name was inscribed there, following his own, for Reb Avraham had no doubt that it was he who would one day serve as his successor, to carry his teachings into the future.

THE TALE OF THE MESSIANIC DREAMS

for Robert A. Cohn

It happened in our time that on the same night three highly respected rabbis of the holy community of Jerusalem dreamed the same apocalyptic dream—that the days of Gog and Magog were upon us, and that the days of the Messiah were close at hand. Word of these three dreams and of the miracle of their coincidence spread rapidly in every *Beit Midrash* and *Beit Knesset* in Jerusalem, and thenceforth was carried abroad to every Jewish community in the world. Discussion of the dreams and their implication dominated every conversation, and the prayers of the Hasidim grew more fervent.

Each and every Hasid was shaken, as if *Yom Kippur* had arrived without warning and he had almost forgotten to fast. Many were stunned at this sudden onset of the final days, and were terrified at the prospect of the dangers of living in the wake of Gog and Magog. True, it was prophesied that in the End of Days Gog and Magog and their armies would fall into the hands of the Messiah, and for seven years the Children of Israel would light fires from their weapons. But the times that would precede the End of Days would be terrible indeed. To what could they be likened? To a man who was walking on a road when he met a wolf and narrowly escaped harm. Then he met a lion, and the lion made him forget the wolf. And, having just escaped from the lion with his life, he met a snake, and the snake made him forget the lion and the wolf as well. And what happened then? If he was one of the fortunate ones he would live to tell the tale of the snake. And if not...

At any time the mountains would begin to tremble, the hills to quake, and the walls and towers to collapse. And just as the Messiah who was on his way would seek them out, so too did the Hasidim prepare themselves to receive him. And every Hasid opened his door in the evening, as is done on *Pesach* for Elijah. And as with Elijah, a cup of wine filled to the brim stood waiting at all times, in case the Redeemer should come to call. And before sleep they would lay out their Sabbath clothes near the bed and lean a pilgrim's staff against them, leaving strict orders to be wakened at the very first sign.

Now it seemed that the Gates of Dream had been opened, and a flood of Messianic dreams convulsed the Hasidic communities. One Reb dreamed that he had seen the Messiah descend to earth by climbing down a tree of light that also seemed to be a ladder. And when this dream was reported it was quickly observed that this must have been Jacob's Ladder, on which Jacob had witnessed angels ascending and descending. For all agreed it was logical for the Messiah to choose to enter the world this way. Soon afterwards, however, another Hasid dreamed that he had seen the Messiah descend to earth like a falling star. And in the dream he had travelled to the place where the star had fallen, and had looked upon the face of the Messiah, but he had been blinded by the light reflected from the Messiah's face, and thus could not describe his features.

Not long afterwards three Hasidim reported that they had looked upon the face of the Messiah in dreams and had not been blinded. And all of them were certain they had recognized the face of the Messiah in their dreams,

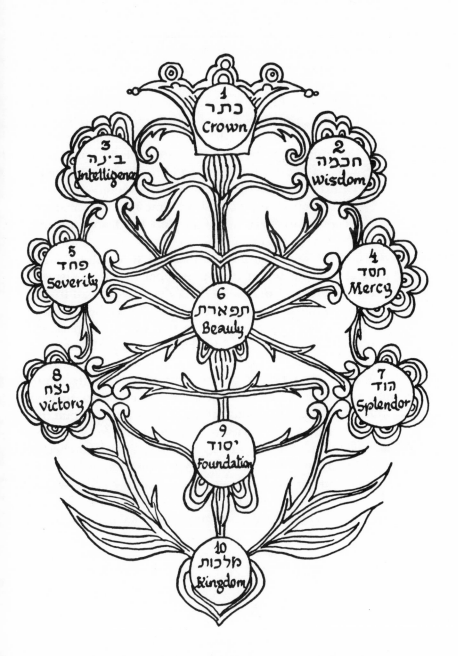

and it was the face of the rabbi who had dreamed of the tree of light that was also a ladder. And this was a certain Reb Yisrael of Meah Shearim.

At first Reb Yisrael was taken aback by this unexpected acclaim, and he seemed to hesitate, but there was no turning back. Not that Reb Yisrael thought of himself as Messiah ben Joseph, who would prepare the way for Messiah ben David, the Redeemer who would initiate the End of Days. But Reb Yisrael had grown impatient for the Coming of the Messiah, and now it seemed to him that the time might be right to hasten the End of Days. For with so many calling out to him, the true Messiah might find it impossible to delay any longer.

So it happened in a very short time that Reb Yisrael was acclaimed in every city of the Holy Land, and prayers were offered in his name, and the fervor of the Hasidim reached the heavens. But the heavens were silent. And only afterwards did anyone remember that Reb Yisrael was a descendant of Joseph de la Reina, who had lived in Safed in the Sixteenth Century. And it was the tragedy of the life of Joseph de la Reina that he was impatient and sought to force the End. For there is a Messiah in every generation, one who is the *Tzaddik ha-dor*, the righteous one whose soul has attained the heights. And he remains hidden until the time has come to reveal himself, if the conditions are right. So did it happen in our days that he who was truly the *Tzaddik ha-dor*, the Messiah in our generation, saw how Reb Yisrael had been acclaimed, and chose not to reveal himself at all, but to remain hidden. In this way the chance to sip the wine that has been saved since before the Creation for the End of Days was lost, the time for the Return had been missed, and it was too late.

THE BLESSING OF THE BLIND REBBE

As Reb Simon stepped through the doorway of the
blind Rebbe's house, the Rebbe said: "Welcome, Yosef!"
"No," said Simon, "my name is not Yosef. It is Simon."
"No," the Rebbe insisted, "you are Yosef, *Mashiah* ben
Yosef, the holy one who will proceed the Redeemer,
Mashiah ben David." These words staggered Reb Simon
as if he had been struck by a sword of fire. For the words
of the Rebbe had to be true—was it not said everywhere
that he, in his blindness, had far better sight than anyone
who could see?

Reb Simon remembered nothing of what had happened
after that. It was as if he too had been struck blind. He,
completely imperfect, one part of triplets, the mirror image of his identical brother—his sister having died from
an imperfect heart; his father struck down by a cossack
when he was only three—had been declared to be the
Tzaddik ha-dor, the Tzaddik of his generation. And the
blind Rebbe had been chosen to deliver this divine message. He did not think overmuch of the end of the prophecy: that Messiah ben Joseph was destined to die before
the arrival of Messiah ben David.

In the following weeks Reb Simon's beard began to grow wild, as wild thoughts invaded him. At first he tried to search for the path on which to reach the one who must already be seeking him out. But the path did not reveal itself, and he soon stopped looking. Instead he was filled to overflowing. He could not bear to keep the secret any longer. But all he chose to confide in either shunned him at once, for good, or else they looked at him and saw him in a new light. Perhaps there was a dim aura surrounding his face. After all, had he not memorized the whole Talmud? (Only Simon knew how he was unable to forget the pages, even when he tried.)

In small groups, in homes, Simon revealed the blind Rebbe's blessing. Those who believed in him sustained him after that. One of them was very rich. After all, it was not as if Simon had declared *himself* to be Messiah ben Yosef. As they considered themselves loyal Hasidim of the blind Rebbe, they followed the path he had pointed out, and it led them to Simon.

The day came when Reb Simon ben Yosef, as his followers called him, decided that he must set out at once for the Holy Land. For surely the End of Days would take place there, and that is where he would find his brother, Messiah ben David. His Hasidim begged him not to go, but secretly they were relieved. They paid his fare.

On the tenth day a storm arose at sea, battering the ship, and driving it onto a great rock, where it shattered. Every passenger lost his life, Reb Simon ben Yosef among them. When the news at last reached Reb Simon's Hasidim, they declared that the prophecy that Messiah ben Joseph would die had been fulfilled. And they said as well that a pure vessel had shattered, because it could not bear such a great light.

THE FALSE REBBE

What started with the proclamation of a new *Tzaddik* among the Hasidim outside Poland soon spread into a sect that crossed into the towns of Poland as well. And Reb Zvi and his Hasidim were very disturbed at the news of this sect, for it was apparent that they were very close to declaring this Rebbe to be the Messiah. And it was quite apparent to Reb Zvi that this man was no Messiah, but, on the contrary, might very well be a blood brother of Shabbatai Zevi, the false Messiah.

Now this Rebbe had been one of the few survivors of a terrible pogrom, but among his Hasidim it came to be said that he was the only survivor—and this was a terrible lie. And among his Hasidim it came to be said that he was also the only victim—to such an extent did they wear blinders that they lost all respect for the truth. And this Rebbe began to assert that he spoke not only for the living, but also for the dead. For he claimed to know the wishes of the dead, whose silence he pretended to interpret. Thus it was apparent to Reb Zvi and all of his Hasidim that this Rebbe was false, and that his Hasidim were nothing more than a band of fools running around in small circles and chanting his name.

Then it happened that this Rebbe came to Buczacz. And Reb Hayim Elya was among those who came to hear him speak on the Sabbath, for Hayim Elya was curious to know the truth about him. And before this Rebbe rose to speak, one of his Hasidim rose and introduced him, and it seemed to Reb Hayim Elya that the face of this man must have closely resembled the face of the Golem of Prague. And when this man spoke of the books his Rebbe had written, he said it was only a question of whether they were the new Midrash or the new Scripture. And he concluded that they were, in fact, the new Scripture. And Reb Hayim Elya could not believe his ears when he heard this. But he was not yet ready to condemn this Rebbe until he had heard him speak for himself.

And then this Rebbe rose to speak. And the first thing he did was to loosen his robe, so that all those present could see the scars of the wounds he had suffered in the pogrom. And then, when he spoke, he compared himself to Moses. And Reb Hayim Elya was as close to him when he said this as one who dines at the table of another, and he was able to confirm that the words had indeed come from his lips. Then anger welled up inside him, and he rose from his place and turned his back on this false Rebbe, and walked away from that place.

And that night Reb Hayim Elya had a remarkable dream. He dreamed that the false Rebbe was actually a child who had managed to escape a pogrom with his life. And an unscrupulous man found him, and decided to exploit his life, and to pretend that the story of the child was actually his own. And the relationship between the child and the man was a very difficult one. On the one hand each depended on the other, but on the other the child came to understand that he was being exploited, and he grew to loathe the one who took advantage of him. And it happened as the child grew older that he longed to escape from the prison of their relationship. And the other was afraid that the child would reveal their secret, and one night he decided to strangle him, to get rid of him once and for all.

And such are the ways of dreams that at the very

moment the false Rebbe entered the room of the child and began to strangle him, Reb Hayim Elya arrived at that place. And he saw what was happening. And the moment the false Rebbe left the child for dead, Reb Hayim Elya rushed in, and summoned a doctor, and helped to bring the child back from the edge of death. And just as they ascertained that the child would live, the false Rebbe burst into the room. He was furious—furious with the child for being alive, and furious with Reb Hayim Elya and the doctor for saving him. And he drew a dagger from under his robe and rushed at Reb Hayim Elya to destroy him.

But at that moment Reb Hayim Elya had a wonderful revelation in that dream. He understood that the false Rebbe, being false, had no power whatsoever. In fact, he was little more than an actor, pretending and playing a role. And no sooner did Reb Hayim Elya come to this understanding than the false Rebbe indeed lost all his power and even the dagger vanished from his hand. Then Hayim Elya felt his anger surge, and he picked up one of the many idols with which the false Rebbe had filled the room, and with that one he smashed all the others and destroyed them. And then he awoke.

THE CANTOR WHO BECAME
AN APOSTATE

It happened in our time that out of a tiny village in Poland there emerged a *hazzan*, a cantor whose song rose up from his soul, and whose ability to blow on the *shofar* was unsurpassed. In a short time his fame spread until he was known in every village and town in Poland and all the rest of *Galut*, and wherever he went he was received with great acclaim. For his voice enabled all the Hasidim who heard him to be carried upward on the wings of song into the realm of the Kingdom of Light.

Now it often happens that the prime of a cantor is a brief one, due to the demands made upon his voice. And when a cantor loses his voice, he loses his livelihood. Yet it happend that the voice of this cantor did not deteriorate, but grew even richer. And in time it also became apparent that this cantor not only had the soul of a *hazzan*, but that of a poet as well, for his lyrics and melodies found favor among the people, and intermingled with the traditional strains, and rarely did a day pass when we were not reminded of him in one way or another. And eventually word of his wonderful singing was carried across the ocean, until it reached the sacred hills and valleys of Jerusalem, and his name was blessed even in the Holy Land.

So moving was the song of this cantor that those who heard him sometimes forgot that he was, after all, a vessel of the Holy One, Blessed be He, and that it was his purpose to be one of those who receive and transmit. For it happened that his fame grew so great that a cult grew up around him, Hasidim who forgot that he was merely the means of reaching the upper realms, and who whispered among themselves that he might even be the Messiah.

So it came to pass that because of this surfeit of honors, and of the strains of travelling from town to town without rest, the cantor began to trust in his own greatness, and came to think of himself as if he were a king. Then it was only the patience and love of his wife, Sarah, that maintained his equilibrium, for she stood firmly on the ground, and was not deluded by fame. So too did she bring into the world four children, each of whom was an abundant blessing. And in the circle of his wife and children the cantor remembered that he was a husband and a father, and did not think of himself as a king.

It happened, inevitably, that the fame of this cantor also came to the attention of the gentiles. One day he received an invitation from the royalty of Poland to perform in their presence, and after that his head again began to swell, and not even his family could reach him, much less his fellow Hasidim. And among those who admired him there were many women, and he was unable to resist their temptations. In this way he came to believe that he no longer cared for his wife, and so after many years of marriage he divorced her and set out alone in his travels from court to court.

Not long afterwards some Hasidim began to note a change taking place both in the cantor's manner and in his singing. No longer did his voice reach the highest heavens, nor could he conceal this fact from those who were sensitive to the *kavanah* of his prayers. And then one day the first of the terrible rumors arrived. It was said that the cantor had been baptised in the lake of a great Polish duke, who had held out great riches to him if he would become an apostate. As this rumor passed from town to town, a great wave of grief convulsed the Hasidim of Poland, and all held out the hope that it might still prove to be false. But when the cantor did not deny this rumor at once, and remained silent, it became apparent that this tragedy must have taken place.

Seeking to bring the cantor to his senses, one reb, an old friend, travelled a great distance to speak to him, but the cantor refused even to meet with him. Shortly afterwards it was announced that the cantor was to sing in a great cathedral. Thus the apostasy was confirmed as a fact, and in the eyes of the Hasidim he became like the false Messiah Shabbatai Zevi—one whose name should be blotted out.

Like many of his fellow Hasidim, Reb Hayim Elya was deeply wounded by this tragedy. Twice in the period following the cantor's conversion he dreamed that he sat among those who listened while he sang Christian hymns, and in both of these dreams Hayim Elya stood up and shouted to the cantor to desist, for he was a Jew. But the cantor turned his face away from him, pretending not to hear his shouts, and continued to sing.

Then one Friday night, after the second of these unhappy dreams, as he sat at the table of Reb Zvi and his Hasidim, Hayim Elya said: "What has happened to this cantor has affected me deeply. For I loved this cantor for many years. I let his voice lead me up the stairs of Jacob's ladder into the heavens. For he was like a guide to me, who never lost the way. Now I see that the guide himself has become lost, and even if I tried to help him it would do no good, so blind has he become. No, now it is apparent that something has broken. But what is it, Rebbe?"

Then Reb Zvi was silent for a long time. But at last he said: "Yes, Hayim Elya, I am afraid that the vessel that once held the splendid light has broken, and cannot be restored. A dangerous soul has come to possess this cantor. This soul was among those that fell most deeply into the abyss of the *klippot*, the empty shells that drag us down into the pit, and make us slaves in Egypt all over again.

"And what soul is it? It is the soul that first possessed Cain, and drove him to kill his brother, Abel. For this soul, which has haunted us throughout the generations, consists only of the *Yetzer Hara*, the evil impulse, and has closed itself completely to the impulse of good, the *Yetzer Tov*. This also was the soul of Esau, that caused him to try to kill his brother Jacob. Later it took over the soul of Elisha ben Abuyah, forcing him to cut the shoots and to become an apostate, and that is why we do not call him by his name, but refer to him as Aher, the Other.

"And this self-same evil soul also took possession of Shabbatai Zevi and convinced him that he was the Messiah, and he, in turn, convinced half the Jews of Europe to follow him across the continent, until the Sultan of Turkey caused him to become an apostate, one who chose to wear the Fez. Now, as you can see, this soul has manifested itself again in our generation.

"But if you listen carefully you will hear the voice of the true soul this cantor has denied crying out from its exile. That is the voice we must help find its way into the world. For even though this cantor has put down the candle it was his destiny to carry, whose flame reaches into Heaven, the flame has not gone out. Before that happens and darkness descends, it is for us to pick up that candle and carry it."

THE TALE OF THE PALACE

for Lyle Harris

Now there was one of Reb Zvi's Hasidim who did not live in Buczacz, but made his home in the nearby town of Kotzk. This was Reb Naftali, who was both a scholar and a wonderful musician. He could play many instruments, but when he played the violin, the music evoked in all who heard it long lost memories of *Gan Eden*, and left those fortunate ones with a taste as sweet as manna. But this Reb Naftali would not pick up an instrument unless he felt that there was a spirit demanding expression. For Reb Naftali was a pure vessel, and the music that flowed from his lips had its source in the spring that flows from the Tree of Life.

As often as possible Reb Naftali made the journey from Kotzk to Buczacz to pray in the synagogue of Reb Zvi. There he listened with great concentration to everything that was said, but more often than not he was silent. When he did speak he often spoke in *moshel*s, for he much admired the Maggid of Dubno, and like the Maggid he chose to couch his understanding of the world in parables.

So it was that one Sabbath Reb Naftali joined Reb Zvi, Reb Hayim Elya and Reb Kalman, and listened as Reb Kalman described a tragedy that had just taken place. A daughter of Israel whose *neshamah* had been counted among the blessed had converted. This conversion, coming as it did on the heels of the conversion of the cantor who had become an apostate, deeply grieved all of the Hasidim, and they fell silent. When at last Reb Kalman spoke again, he said: "What upsets me most of all is that these *Mashumadim*, these apostates, have taken what they have been given, which belongs to all of us, and given it away to strangers, none of whom will know what it is worth."

Then Reb Naftali spoke for the first time that day and said: "You must remember, Reb Kalman, that this is not the first time such a thing has happened. But let me tell it to you as a tale:

"Once there was a great king who had a dream in which he entered a magnificent palace and explored every passage and chamber. And when he awoke he recalled every detail of that palace, and summoned the greatest architect in his kingdom. As the king described the palace, the architect wrote down everything he said, then drew up plans for a palace such as the king had described. And when the king saw that the plans were true to his dream in the smallest detail, he gave the order that the palace should be built. And that was a great undertaking, which required the labor of an army of workers. Nor was it completed in one generation, but each succeeding generation had the honor of perfecting another aspect of that wonderful palace.

"Then it happened that in one of these generations there was a worker, who was only one of many, who took one of the stones of the wall that was being built around the palace, and carried it away and gave it to strangers from another kingdom. And that worker told the strangers that the stone he brought them had come from one of the innermost chambers, and when they saw how finely carved it was, they were seized by the desire to build a palace of their own, one that would be even

more beautiful than the palace of the king. How could they know that the king's palace had been built according to his dream? How could they know that the form of that dream-palace was perfect, and could not be improved upon?

"Now the truth was that this workman had never stepped foot inside the palace at all. His knowledge was limited to what he obtained while working on the wall that surrounded it. Nonetheless, hearing him describe the palace the strangers were convinced that he knew enough of the secret for them to construct their own palace on the basis of that partial knowledge, and that is what they proceeded to do.

"They took the stone that the workman had brought to them, and made it the cornerstone of the edifice they intended to construct. But because they knew almost nothing of the art of construction, they threw in everything they could find to make the mortar—sand, mud, wood, and scraps of various kinds, mixed with rough rocks. And because they wanted to complete the entire edifice in one generation, they took little care in building the foundation, which remained partial and incomplete. For they preferred to imagine the upper reaches, and all were willing to sacrifice what was below for what was above.

"After years of building they succeeded at last in constructing an enormous edifice, but no sooner did they think it had been completed than they discovered that it was falling apart. The foundation had been reduced to rubble, and almost immediately the structure began to sink. Every year it continued to sink another story into the earth, and they worked furiously to add new stories at the top, but the builders were hard pressed to maintain the number of stories it had reached before it began to sink.

"In this way these people were like the builders of the Tower of Babel, who ignored the signs warning them not to try to climb any higher, for danger of a great fall. They thought only of the immense shadow such an edifice would cast, for they became obsessed with the thought that such a shadow should reach around the world.

"And when the structure was erected, the people told themselves that it was even more beautiful than the palace of the king, even though they had never seen that palace. For there was a law among them that made it forbidden to pass beyond the outer wall that surrounded it. And all they knew of the king's palace came from those who heard it described by the workman who brought them the stone in the first place, and even this became distorted over the generations. And in time legends grew up about that workman. It was forgotten that he had been one of many workers, and instead it was believed that he had been the chief architect.

"Yet the truth remained: Beneath the weak foundation there was still that one precious stone, one seed of truth, obscured by all the rubble. But those builders could not imagine how a stone could also serve as a seed, nor did they ever discover how to make that seed sprout—it has remained barren until this day.

"As for the palace of the King, hidden and recondite as it is, and concealed from the gaze of outsiders by the great wall, it continues to exist in all its glory, and has continued to reveal new secrets to those in each generation who have explored its multitude of passages and chambers, as well as to serve those who prefer to remain within the presence of the Throne, where the descendants of the first king continue to guide their subjects with the wisdom and mercy of the original ruler."

REB HAYIM ELYA
CONSULTS AN ORACLE

Like his father and his grandfather before him, Reb Hayim Elya was a Cohen, and thus traced his descent from the High Priests of the Temple. In the time of the Temple, the priests wore a breastplate called *Urim Ve' Thummim*. Attached to that breastplate were twelve stones with which the priests were able to divine. But after the destruction of the Temple the gift of prophecy was lost, as was the secret of how to read the oracle in the stones of the breastplate.

Now Hayim Elya was a pious man, who performed as many *mitzvot* as he could. But in one thing he was seriously deficient, for he persisted in searching for signs from Heaven and in the reading of oracles of all kinds. He was unable to restrain himself, perhaps because the gift of prophecy had not fully been lost to him. True, only a small part of it remained. Such a small part that it was useless to try to hear directly the commands of the Holy One, as could the prophets. Instead he was driven to consult oracles, from witches to water, from cloud forms to stars, from fire to ice.

One day Hayim Elya was walking in the forest by himself. Later that evening he was to study alone with Reb Zvi, and he looked forward to these meetings, for much had been clarified since they began. Now, when Hayim Elya looked down, he saw the shell of a turtle on the floor of the forest, and from the instant he saw it he was seized by the desire to burn that shell in a fire, and to read from it the cracks in the shell, that would reveal the turnings of the future. And without hesitating he gathered firewood and built a fire in that place, and cast the shell into the fire, and watched carefuly as it burned. And although he had never in his life seen a tortoise-shell cracked in fire, when Hayim Elya saw the first cracks that appeared on that shell he was able to read them as if they were words. And with each subsequent crack the message became clearer and more certain, and Hayim Elya became frightened. For the message that was written there was clearly one of warning, of a danger that threatened. And as this was the meaning of the first cracks that formed, so it was repeated by the last cracks in the shell.

When Hayim Elya recovered from his initial fright, he attempted to clarify where the danger lay. He tried to remember what he was thinking when he had come across the shell. And he recalled that he had been think- ing about Reb Zvi. And because all signs revealed them- selves to him that day as if they spoke a common language, he understood that the shell must have been sent to answer a question. And what was the question? Well, it must concern Reb Zvi, since it was Reb Zvi he was thinking of when he chanced upon it. So the warn- ing of danger might be directed toward Reb Zvi, or perhaps toward his relationship with Reb Zvi. When Hayim Elya realized this he grew fearful that some trag- ic rent in their relationship might be imminent. Such a thought was unthinkable to him, yet he sensed that the danger was real, for he truly discerned its presence. And Hayim Elya became as one who is paralyzed, and he was afraid to turn back and return, yet he knew at the same time that the warning must be heeded.

Then Hayim Elya thought that even if he gave the warn- ing, Reb Zvi would reject it because he abhorred the reading of oracles. He did not regard them as pure gates, and he was unwilling to accept messages from impure gates.

With great shame, Hayim Elya realized that his doubts were causing him to lose valuable time, that he must hurry back to Reb Zvi and warn him of the danger. And it was then that he became aware that he had wandered freely through the forest while considering the meaning of the oracle; nor had he paused to take note of his way. Thus he had become lost in the forest, and he did not even know where to begin to find his way back.

Almost at once the sun vanished from the sky; Hayim Elya did not even see it set. It was dark in that forest, and Hayim Elya, who was not a madman, knew he might not survive the night if he stayed on the floor of the forest; he must sleep in the branches of a tree or else serve as food for the wolves that wandered there at night. And with the greatest regret and confusion, Hayim Elya recognized that he must put off his return and his warning to Reb Zvi until the next morning. Nor did he sleep a wink that whole night, but the baying of the wolves sent shivers through his body, as did his fears for Reb Zvi, and he spent the night in prayer and supplication.

At the very moment the first thin crest of the sun showed in the sky, Hayim Elya climbed down from the branches, said the morning prayers, and ran as fast as he could in the direction his heart told him to run, for there were no other signs for him to follow. With all his strength and determination he ran, and in this way he reached a clearing that was familiar, and he knew he was no longer lost. Then he hurried out of the forest and came to the House of Study.

When Hayim Elya arrived he saw from the window that Reb Zvi's Hasidim were quite agitated. He was afraid that they thought him lost or dead, but when he entered the House of Study one Hasid gave him an angry look and said: "Where have you been? We have been praying all night for Reb Zvi's unborn child." Hayim Elya gasped and said: "What has happened to the child?" For he knew well that Reb Zvi's wife was carrying a child in the eighth month. And the other said: "Is it possible that you do not know? Yesterday Reb Zvi's wife was injured when

her horse stumbled and the carriage overturned. Everyone was afraid for the life of the child. And it was a time of torture until the doctor arrived, and told us that the heart of the child was still beating. And we all gave thanks. And now we have decided to hold a vigil for the next month, until the child is born, so that our prayers may protect the child from any further danger."

And when Hayim Elya heard the word "danger," he almost fainted. For he remembered the oracle of the tortoise-shell, and the message of danger he had failed to deliver. Then Hayim Elya ran from the House of Study to the home of Reb Zvi, and prostrated himself before him, and told him the whole story, and begged to be forgiven for having failed to deliver the message of danger.

And when Reb Zvi had listened to what Hayim Elya had said, he replied: "First of all, do not hold yourself responsible for what has happened, Hayim Elya. Even if you had delivered the warning there is nothing that could have been done. Who could have known that a horse would stumble? It is foolish to try to alter fate.

"Then you must see this as I do, and thank God that despite such a severe accident the heart of the child is still beating.

"Again, to be honest, I might have rejected the warning because of the source. For I abhor the reading of oracles, and I only wish to receive messages that come through the gates of purity."

"Finally, yes, there is a mystery here, Hayim Elya. But perhaps this is one mystery that we would be better off not to pursue any further. In the future, do not tell me if you consult an oracle. But if the message you receive is intended for me, deliver it as a message of your own, and in that case I will not fail to heed what you say."

THE SACRED RAM

One day Reb Hayim Elya said to Reb Zvi: "Tell me, Rebbe, what happened to the Shofar that was made from the horn of the ram that Abraham sacrificed at Mount Moriah in place of Isaac, his son?"

Reb Zvi said: "Close your eyes, Hayim Elya."

Hayim Elya closed his eyes.

"Now tell me what you see," said Reb Zvi.

Hayim Elya said: "I see a field."

Reb Zvi said: "How many trees are there in that field."

Hayim Elya said: "There is only one tree, in the center of the field, which has a long trunk and a great many branches."

Reb Zvi said: "Do you see anything else?"

Hayim Elya said: "Yes, now I see a ram coming over the hill. It has long, twisting horns that are wonderous to behold."

Then Reb Zvi said: "Look closely, Hayim Elya, for those are the horns of the very ram about which you asked."

And Hayim Elya closed his eyes even tighter to take a better look at that fabulous ram, but at that instant the vision ended, and he saw nothing but after-images.

Yet that night, in a dream, Hayim Elya was able to continue his search for the sacred ram after all. He was travelling to the place where he had seen it in his vision. He was certain that if he could find the ram, and perhaps capture it, he would become the master of many mysteries. And no sooner did he reached the place in the desert that he believed to be its home, than rain struck with great force, and a river rose up and carried him off and set him down on a desert island that had been formed when all the land surrounding it had been flooded. Nothing was to be seen there except for a single tree that grew in the center of the island. Then, all at once, he saw a giant ram approaching him at great speed, with its horns lowered. At that moment Hayim Elya did not consider that this might be the sacred ram he was seeking, but rather sought refuge in the one place available, the tree.

Using one overhanging branch to secure his grip, Hayim Elya managed to swing into the tree and then proceeded to climb to the top of the branches just as the ram arrived at the base of the tree. From his refuge he saw that the eyes of the ram were remarkably like those of a human being, and that the ram was in a terrible temper because Hayim Elya had escaped. Then Hayim Elya said a silent prayer giving thanks for having managed to save himself under the circumstances. But the ram was not about to turn back. To Hayim Elya's amazement it started to climb up the trunk of the tree, shinnying upward in a way unlike that of any other animal. In this manner the ram came quite close and Hayim Elya realized that he was about to be overrun when, in his desperation, he clutched for what was nearest, a cluster of seed-like pebbles he found in a hollow of the tree. Using these to ward off the ram, Hayim Elya threw the pebbles as soon as the ram was within striking distance. And though the stone seemed insignificant and the effort hopeless, in fact the pebbles caused the ram to lose its grip and slip rapidly to the base of the tree, where it struck the ground with such great force that for a moment Hayim Elya was afraid that the tree itself might be uprooted.

Looking down from his perch, Hayim Elya was certain that the ram had not survived the fall. But just as he

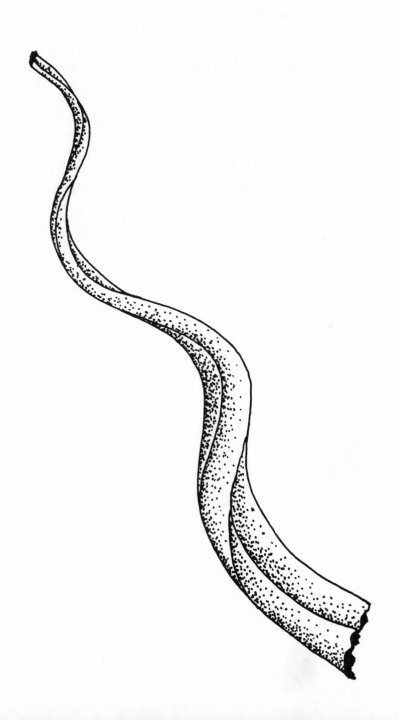

breathed a sigh of relief, the ram twitched and gave signs of coming back to life. Then Hayim Elya grew frantic and reached into the hollow for another handful of pebbles, but he discovered that his only weapon had blossomed into soft, beautiful flowers. Meanwhile, at the base of the tree, the ram had revived and was about to make another effort to climb the trunk. And Hayim Elya only managed to elude a confrontation by waking from his dream at that moment.

That morning, when Hayim Elya met with Reb Zvi, Reb Zvi smiled at him and said: "Tell me, Hayim Elya, what happened to the Shofar that was made from the horn of the ram that Abraham sacrificed at Mount Moriah in place of Isaac, his son?"

THE POWER OF PRAYER

for Maury Schwartz

When Reb Hayim Elya was still a boy, about a year before his *Bar Mitzvah*, the time drew near for his mother to give birth again. When the birth pains began, Reb Nussan, her husband and the father of Hayim Elya, went to inform the doctor and brought him home with him to deliver the child.

After the doctor had been in the bedroom for what seemed many hours, he came out looking sad and exhausted, and told Reb Nussan that the birth was going very badly, and that it appeared that the lives of both the child and the mother hung in the balance and might be lost.

When he heard this the world around Reb Nussan became a great blur and he stumbled from the house with his younger brother, Reb Moshe, who lived nearby. Together they went to the *Beit Knesset*, which was empty at that hour, where Reb Nussan prayed.

According to Reb Moshe, who was present in that place, Reb Nussan prostrated himself before the Ark and prayed fervently for the lives of his wife and child. He threw himself upon the mercy of the Holy One, blessed be He, and promised to dedicate himself even more to the fulfillment of the commandments. Never in his life had Reb Moshe witnessed such passion from one who prayed, and the sight of it reduced him to tears.

Afterwards the two brothers came back to Reb Nussan's home. There they were met by the doctor, who was beaming—"Both mother and child are safe," he said as they entered, "I can't explain it. Perhaps a miracle has taken place."

THE SILVER TREE

In Memory of Nathan Schwartz

Before his death Reb Nussan had a dream in which he looked outside the window of his house and there he saw a silver tree. Not believing his eyes, he hurried outside to see if such a thing were possible. And when he went out the door he saw that a silver tree had indeed taken root in front of his house. Now in that dream Reb Nussan was not a jeweler, who cut and polished precious gems; rather he was a silversmith, whose work it was to hammer out the silver crowns for the Torah known as *rimonim*. And as he stood beside that silver tree he saw that its fruit were such pear-shaped crowns, beaten from the finest silver and polished until they shone like mirrors. So too did its silver trunk reflect images, although not those of a mirror. Instead it reflected a vision of a garden surrounded by a mist. And as the mist began to clear, Reb Nussan saw a river take form that soon branched off into four streams, one in each direction, which watered that garden and made it fertile.

And all at once Reb Nussan looked down and saw that

he was being borne on those waters as if he were in a boat, although he was not. And that boat had set sail on the river flowing North, whose waters were silver, like the silver tree.

And when he recalled that tree, Reb Nussan found himself standing before it once again. And he only managed to glimpse it for an instant before he realized that he must be dreaming and woke up.

Now that day was *Simhat Torah*, on which scrolls of the Torah are carried around the synagogue. And that year Reb Nussan was called upon to carry the Torah, even though he was an old man. Nor had he ever let the torch of the Torah fall from his grasp. And as Reb Nussan clung to the Torah, its silver *rimonim* shimmered before his eyes, as close as he had been to the fruit of the silver tree. And at that moment Reb Nussan understood that the fruit of the Torah can be found in all worlds, in this one and in the *Yenne Velt* as well. And suddenly Reb Nussan felt light, as if it were the Torah that were carrying him, rather than he who held it in his grasp.

THE MINYAN

One of the last wishes of Reb Nussan, father of Reb Hayim Elya, before he died, was that Hayim Elya should say the *Kaddish,* the prayer for the dead, in the same *minyan* where Reb Nussan had prayed for so many years. This Hayim Elya undertook to do. And so it was that each day he prayed *Shahareis, minhah* and *Ma'ariv* with the old men who made up that *minyan,* led by a *hazzan,* since they did not have a rabbi of their own.

And in that tiny *Beit Knesset* it was a struggle every day to assemble a *minyan.* In the winter, especially, there were many days when the old men had to wait hours while one of them went in search of a tenth man. And when he saw how the old men had to struggle before they could begin their prayers, Reb Hayim Elya understood why his father had wanted him to pray in that place.

Now in addition to Reb Hayim Elya and the old men, there was also one man—young in comparison to the others—who always prayed in that *minyan.* The son of this man had been killed while serving in a Duke's army, and the man had never recovered. Before this happened he had never been known to be observant. But afterward he began to serve as a *shammes* and became one of the pillars of the *minyan*.

Also there was a woman who was always present, strange as that may sound. This woman, whose name was Bracha, which means "Blessing," showed up for every service—at the crack of dawn and when the sun was about to set. And she always stood in the hallway outside the door of the House of Prayer, and never came inside, for this *Beit Knesset* was so small that no place had been set aside for women.

From the old men Reb Hayim Elya learned that this woman had stopped speaking when her mother had died, almost ten years before. Although she could not be counted in the *minyan*, the old men believed she came back to hear them pray the *Kaddish*, as did the father who had never stopped mourning for his son. And during the rest of the day she wandered around Buczacz and sometimes wandered in the forest, and her life was a lonely one.

Now in this *minyan* there was a slight struggle that always took place among the old men. For it happened that the *hazzan* loved to sing the *Kaddish*, for he much loved a beautiful melody. Yet among the rest of the old men they preferred to chant the *Kaddish*, to emphasize its strong rhythm. So it often happened that each would try to start the prayer a little before the other. And if the *hazzan* started to sing first, he would pull the others into the song; but if the old men started to chant first, then the *hazzan* joined them in chanting. And this little tug of war was hidden, and was not even acknowledged. But in the eleven months he prayed in that *minyan*, Reb Hayim Elya came to notice that when one side managed to start a little sooner and pulled the other along with them, then the *Kaddish* was harmonious, and it seemed to him that the prayer reached the angels. But when both sides started at the same time, and neither would give way, then the prayer failed to ascend to the other side.

Before long, Reb Hayim Elya also became aware that on the days when their prayers reached the celestial realms, the face of the woman Bracha was glowing as he left the House of Prayer, as if surrounded by an aura of

light. But on those days when the prayers were restrained as if by strong cords, and never left this world, then the face of the woman was empty, without light. And on the days when their prayers strained to reach the lowest of the heavens, a light would be present in her face, but it would be dim.

Once he had observed this, Reb Hayim Elya made it his practice to measure for himself the level of *kedushah* their prayers achieved, and then to study Bracha's face as he departed, and in this way he confirmed that there was a complete correlation between their prayers and the presence or absence and degree of the light that shone from her face.

So it was that morning, afternoon and evening, Bracha offered all their prayers her silence, and when they turned to go, the light that surrounded her face measured their distance from the angels they called to carry back their prayers for the departed, and to bring them their blessings in return.

THE LOST WILL

At the time of the death of Reb Yehezkel, no will had been found. The search for it was extensive, and in the process many lost things were recovered, but not the will. This was a matter of great importance because it was known that in it Reb Yehezkel had revealed where he had hidden a bag of golden coins, his life savings.

Hayim Elya was a boy at the time of his grandfather's death, and he did not fully understand the desperation with which all members of the family searched for his grandfather's will. And as he grew older he began to wonder if the bag of gold coins truly existed. But on this matter there seemed little doubt among the other members of the family. For at one point Reb Yehezkel showed a bag of such coins to his wife and eldest son, Reb Nussan, explaining that he intended to hide the bag, and would reveal the hiding place in his will. At the time, of course, no one imagined that the will itself could become lost.

Many years passed and Reb Nussan, Hayim Elya's father, died. But still the will remained lost. Then it happened during the Days of Awe between Rosh Hashanah and Yom Kippur that Hayim Elya dreamt about the lost will. In the dream Reb Nussan told him that the missing will was to be found in one of the books that belonged to his father, Reb Yehezkel. And in the dream Reb Nussan showed Hayim Elya which book it was. Then he told Hayim Elya that he was giving him the task of executing the will. After that Hayim Elya awoke.

Now when Hayim Elya recalled this dream and the title of the book in which Reb Nussan said the will could be found, he arose and went to that book, which now belonged to him. For he had inherited that book among those that had belonged to his father, as his father had inherited it from his father before him. Hayim Elya took down the book and turned through its pages, and lo and behold, a sealed envelope fell out. With trembling hands Hayim Elya opened the envelope, and there he found the lost will of his grandfather and read the secret of where the bag of gold had been hidden.

Naturally Hayim Elya was overwhelmed to make such a discovery. Even without the matter of the gold coins, finding the will after all those years was remarkable, to say the least. But at the same time Hayim Elya recalled that in the dream he had been charged with executing the will, and now that responsibility hung over him as heavily as did the potential reward of finding the golden coins lost for so long. Thus Hayim Elya read the will slowly, word by word, trying to recapture in this way the sense of his grandfather's voice and presence in those words written so long ago. And there Hayim Elya read Reb Yehezkel's legacy and the secret of the lost inheritance.

And then Hayim understood why his father, Reb Nusan, had charged him with executing the will, for when he read where the golden coins had been hidden, he understood that retrieving them would be no simple task. Reb Yehezkel had buried the coins beneath a tree on land that had once belonged to him. But that land had been sold long ago, and now it belonged to another. Perhaps the gold could no longer be said to belong to the family of Hayim Elya; in any case Hayim Elya would have to obtain permission from the new land owners to recover it.

Another man might have gone there in the dead of night and dug beneath that tree, but Hayim Elya would not stoop to do such a thing. No, he had been charged by his departed father to complete this task, and thus it had to be done in the proper way.

So it was that Hayim Elya went to the house of the family who now lived on that land, which once belonged to his grandfather. The people, whom he had not seen in many years, remembered him well, and asked about his family, and reminisced about the past. At last Hayim Elya told them the tale of the lost will. And when they heard that he had recovered the will through a dream, they agreed at once that if the treasure were to be found on their land, it would belong to the family of Hayim Elya, since it was intended for them alone. That is, the parents agreed to this. But among their children there was one, a daughter, who vehemently disagreed. She insisted that if the gold were buried on their property, then it belonged to them, and to them alone. Hayim Elya saw the anger and hatred in her eyes and said nothing. But no matter how hard she insisted, her parents remained convinced that if anything were found beneath that tree, its discovery was due to a miracle. And being pious Jews they did not wish to take possession of something not intended for them. For who knows how the souls of the dead will take revenge if they are cheated? In the end Hayim Elya was given permission to search for the gold beneath that tree, and if he found it, it belonged to him alone.

Then, with great trepidation, Hayim Elya went to the tree described in Reb Yehezkel's will. And he dug in the very place his grandfather had described, so long ago. Then, no more than one foot beneath the earth, he struck something hard. And when he dug it out, he found a small chest buried there. Inside the chest he found a bag filled with golden coins, just as the will provided. And in that moment Hayim Elya exulted, not only because the lost inheritance had been recovered, but because his grandfather's will had been executed at last, after so many years.

Then, out of gratefulness for the generosity of the

family who had renounced their rights to that treasure, he gave them a tithe of it, which was a substantial reward in itself. And then he gathered together all of the members of his family and revealed the dream and the discovery of the will and the lost inheritance to them, and read the will to them from beginning to end, and they were all astonished. And after that Hayim Elya divided the inheritance equally among all of them, as his grandfather and father would have wished. And Hayim Elya felt great relief and happiness, not only for the treasure that had been lost and recovered, but for the lost words that had been found as well. And he knew that somewhere the souls of his father and grandfather shared his joy, for at last the terms of the will had been fulfilled.

THE TWELFTH PALACE

for Marc Bregman

As he walked to the synagogue on the eve of the twelfth *yahrzeit* of his father, Reb Nussan, Hayim Elya noticed that the skies had grown grey as if a snowfall were imminent. Among those who had already gathered there were Reb Moshe, younger brother of Reb Nussan, and his son, David, who had recently reached the age of *Bar Mitzvah.* Hayim Elya joined them, although they spoke little, for their thoughts concerned Reb Nussan, whose departure twelve year ago still seemed so recent. Soon the *minyan* prayed *Minhah* and then resumed the *Shiur,* the study-session between the evening prayers, while they awaited the three stars that indicated night had fallen.

For several months those in the *minyan* had been studying the tractate *Hagigah* of the Talmud during the *Shiur,* and they had almost finished it. Now they completed the final portion while young David, the son of Reb Moshe, went outside periodically to see if the required three stars had yet appeared. The first time he went out no stars were to be seen. The second time he glimpsed a single star, and the third time he saw a second star glimmering nearby it. But by then the *minyan* had completed their study of *Hagigah*, and still it was not time to resume the service.

Then Reb Zvi suggested that they spend the remaining time studying a midrash, and asked Hayim Elya, who was standing closest to the door of the *Beit Midrash*, to go inside and bring back a book. But when Hayim Elya stepped inside the House of Study he found that it was dark, since the lamp had not been lit. And since little time remained before the final star would appear, he did not light the lamp, but simply approached the bookshelves and took down a large book at random from the section he knew held the books of the Midrash. And he brought that book back into the House of Prayer.

When he had returned, Reb Zvi asked him what book he had brought. Then Hayim Elya looked at its spine, but the name of the book was no longer to be found there. So he opened to the title page and found that he had selected an edition of the *Midrash Tanhuma*, with a commentary by Moshe ben Yitzhak HaPardesan. When he noted this Reb Zvi nodded and asked him to read them a midrash. Then Hayim Elya opened the book at random and began to read: "Let our Master teach us. How long is the judgment of the wicked in Gehenna? Our rabbis taught: The judgment of the wicked in Gehenna is twelve months, while the souls of the righteous hover near their graves for the first twelve months, to remain near those that they have left behind."

Here Reb Zvi stopped Hayim Elya and asked him to read from the commentary. And the commentary said: "The number twelve is of great importance in regard to the souls of the dead. For the souls of the wicked are punished in Gehenna for a maximum of twelve months. Most, however remain in Gehenna only for eleven months, for only the most wicked have to remain there the full twelve months. And this is the reason the *Kaddish* is only recited for the first eleven months, since every man must assume that his father is not among the most wicked. And after that, *Kaddish* is said on every *Yahrzeit*.

"Yet the number twelve is important in another

respect. For the soul of a righteous man remains in this world, hovering near its grave, for the first eleven months after his death, and then begins a slow ascent. And on the first *Yahrzeit*, if the *Kaddish* of the son is said with complete *kavanah*, then the *neshamah* is lifted up, as if on the wings of the *Shekhinah*, into the first palace of heaven. For there are twelve palaces in Paradise for the souls of the righteous. And on each subsequent *Yahrzeit*, with the aid of the *Kaddish,* the souls of the righteous are elevated into the next heavenly palace.

"Now many righteous souls are to be found in the first eleven heavenly palaces. But just as few are so wicked as to require punishment in Gehenna for the full twelve months, so rare too are those souls which succeed in attaining the twelfth palace. For the *kavanah* of the descendents is rarely that intense or that long-lasting that by the twelfth year it is as great as it was on the first *Yahrzeit*. For with each passing year, as the righteous soul is elevated to each succeeding palace, the *neshamah* becomes increasingly remote from this world. And that is why it is so difficult for those left behind to sustain that level of *kavanah*. In the Zohar it is written that the twelfth palace is the most mysterious and recondite of all, as unknown as is the *Ein Sof*. But I have heard from my sainted father, Reb Yitzhak ben Moshe, may his soul rest in the highest palace, that, in fact, the twelfth palace completes the circle, bringing the soul even closer to this world than when it hovered near its grave."

Here the commentary ended, and all the Hasidim agreed that it greatly illuminated the mitzvah of the *Kaddish* on each *Yahrzeit* and revealed its great significance. Just then young David returned from outside, and reported that the third star had finally appeared, and the Minyan began at once to pray *Ma'ariv*. And when the time came to say the Mourner's *Kaddish,* Hayim Elya recited it with complete *kavanah*, for the words of the commentary had spoken more directly to him than to any other, since that was the very day of the twelfth *Yahrzeit* of his father.

As Hayim Elya left the synagogue that night, walking with Reb Moshe and his son David, he saw that it had begun to snow. The flakes fell thick and heavy, and Hayim Elya worried that if they fell all night it would be difficult to reach the synagogue in time for *Shahareis*, and that he must wake earlier to be certain not to miss saying *Kaddish* on that crucial *Yahrzeit*.

That night Hayim Elya slept fitfully, waking at least once an hour, for he dared not oversleep. Each time he got out of bed, went over to the window, and looked outside. And each time he saw that the snow was still falling, as heavy as ever. This continual waking up took its toll on him, and when only two hours remained before it was time to arise, he fell into a deep sleep, and had a vivid dream.

In the dream he woke up and saw that the light outside was grey, and understood that the sun was about to rise and that he had overslept. Then he jumped up, put on his clothes, grabbed his *tallis* and *tefillin*, and ran outside. That is when he discovered that the snow that had been falling all night covered his yard and the roof of his house, at least twelve inches deep, but it had completely vanished everywhere else! Hayim Elya could not understand this at all, but he was so afraid of missing the *Kaddish* that he dashed off to the synagogue at once.

As he ran, however, Hayim Elya thought about the snow he had seen around his house, but nowhere else. He wondered how all the other snow had melted so quickly and what it meant that it remained solely there. And the thought crossed his mind that it might be an evil sign, since snow falls in the winter, and winter is the season of death. Then, when he had almost reached the synagogue, he suddenly realized that although he had taken along his *tallis* and *tefillin*, he had forgotten to put on his *yarmulke*. This horrified him, for there was no time to go back for it, and he abhorred the thought of entering the *Beit Knesset* without it. But there was no time to turn back, so he hurried on, more anxious than ever, to the synagogue.

Somehow the sunrise, which had seemed imminent when he had awakened, had not yet taken place, and Hayim Elya began to hope that he might reach the synagogue in time. When he was almost there, however, he saw to his amazement that its roof and yard too, were covered with snow, exactly as was Hayim Elya's home. Yet there was no snow to be seen anywhere else—not on the path, nor in the fields, nor on the trees. Then, just beyond the door of the synagogue, Hayim Elya saw something in the snow. He bent down and pulled it out, and found, to his great delight, that it was a snow-white *yarmulke*. He quickly put it on his head and entered the synagogue.

But no sooner did he step inside the House of Study, which led to the House of Prayer, than Hayim Elya discovered that something strange had take place. The

Beit Midrash was still darkened and no one was to be seen. Yet even in the dark the room seemed transformed and Hayim Elya seemed to make out an object inside that seemed to resemble a bed. Just then the grey light in the room grew brighter, and he saw that it was indeed a bed, with a woman asleep upon it! She lay there with her face turned away, so that only her long, dark hair could be seen. This sight completely astounded Hayim Elya, but he had no time to consider it, for as soon as the light touched the face of the woman, she awoke and when she saw Hayim Elya standing there, she smiled. And when Hayim Elya saw that smile, all of his anxiety and confusion vanished, and he was filled with peace. Then the woman sat up on the bed, and that is when Hayim Elya realized that he recognized her, although he could not recall ever having met her before in his life. The woman, still smiling, stood up and walked across the room to the door that led to the House of Prayer. With her gaze still fixed on Hayim Elya, she opened the door and indicated that he should enter there. And Hayim Elya did not hesitate, but stepped inside through the doorway, wondering greatly what he would find within.

But no sooner had he crossed that threshold, than Hayim Elya was suddenly blinded by a great light, and at first he could see nothing at all. Yet soon his eyes began to grow accustomed to that sudden illumination, and he was able to make out that it was streaming forth from behind the Pargod, the curtain hanging before the Ark. For an instant Hayim Elya had an overwhelming desire to pull the curtain aside, to see what was the source of that great light. But almost at the same time he realized that this could be a grave error, and that staring into the source of that light might be blinding, like staring into the eye of the sun. And as he gazed upon that light that streamed forth from within the Ark, a vague presence began to take form before his eyes, as if a veil had been lifted. Yet he still could not discern what it was that he saw, only that he felt nourished in its presence, as if he fed off the glory of that light. And while he stared at that mysterious presence, he came to know a peace deeper than he had ever known, and he sighed a great sigh of relief. And at that very moment he awoke.

When Hayim Elya found that he had been dreaming, he could not believe it at first, so vivid and real had the dream been. And while the glow of that mysterious light still filled him, he saw to his distress that the light outside was grey and quickly growing lighter, and understood that he had overslept, just as he had in the dream. Then Hayim Elya dressed in an instant, not forgetting his *yarmulke*, and hurried off with his *tallis* and *tefillin*. But when he stepped outside he saw that it was the entire landscape that was covered with a foot of snow, not only his own house and yard. And, as the first rays of the sun peered above the horizon he ran through that deep snow towards the synagogue.

When Hayim Elya reached the synagogue he was afraid to go inside at first, recalling his dream, but he did not let himself hesitate, and when he entered the House of Study he found it the same as always, filled with a great many old texts, and from the House of Prayer he heard the first words of the opening prayer, for the Hasidim had waited for him as long as they could, and now they were beginning to pray. Then Hayim Elya quickly huried inside, took his place, and put on his *tallis* and *tefillin*. And no sooner did he open the *siddur* than the *minyan* began to chant the Mourner's *Kaddish,* and Hayim Elya was able to join in with the others. And with the glow of that mysterious dream still within him, Hayim Elya had no difficulty cleaving to the intention of his prayer. And when the service had ended, he knew that he had indeed prayed with the necessary *kavanah*.

All that day Hayim Elya thought over that dream and the fact that it was his father's twelfth *Yahrzeit*. And he concluded that all that had taken place pointed to the possibility that his own father's soul was poised to enter into the twelfth palace, of which the commentary on *Midrash Tanhuma* had spoken. And he realized he must sustain that level of *kavanah* for the final reciting of the *Kaddish* during *Minhah* that night. For that was the last time *Kaddish* had to be recited for the *Yahrzeit*. And Hayim Elya resolved to remain in the center of peace to which he had arrived.

That day Hayim Elya was the most agreeable of men. No one, not even those who might have wished it, succeeded in provoking him in any way. And all that day he carried with him the blessing of peace he had known as he stood before the mysterious light emanating from the Ark. So too was that one of the most beautiful days in memory. The sun came out much more strongly than could have been expected, and the snow, in a great rush, began to melt.

So it was that by the time Hayim Elya set off for the synagogue late in the afternoon, the snow had completely vanished. Yet, to his amazement, it still remained covering the roof of his house, as it had in his dream. And when he reached the synagogue he saw to his eternal joy that the roof of the synagogue, too, was covered with snow, so that both were pure white, like the snow-white *yarmulke* he had found in his dream. And then he knew with certainty that the snow was not a sign of danger, but one of purity and affirmation.

And when Hayim Elya stood for the Mourner's *Kaddish* and prayed, the words rose up from within as if on wings. And when he departed from the synagogue that night he knew beyond doubt that his prayers had been sufficient and that the soul of his father had indeed been elevated to the twelfth heavenly palace.

GLOSSARY

(All terms are Hebrew except where noted)

Aggada—The body of Jewish legends; specifically, those found in the Talmud and Midrash.

Akedah—The binding of Isaac by Abraham on Mount Moriah.

Bar Mitzvah—The ceremony at which a boy of 13 is formally accepted into the adult Jewish community.

Barchu es Adonai hamevorach—The opening lines of an important prayer which means "Bless the Lord who is to be blessed."

Baruch HaShem—An expression of affirmation, literally, "Bless the Name," referring to the Name of God.

Bat Kol—Literally, "sister of the voice." An idiom for a voice that speaks forth from the heavens.

Beit Knesset—The House of Prayer.

Beit Midrash—The House of Study. Usually a separate room or building beside the House of prayer.

Besht—An acronym for the *Baal Shem Tov*, the founder of Hasidism.

Bimah—The Pulpit, where the prayer leader prays.

Daven—To pray.

Drash—The third level of the system of biblical interpretation known as *Pardes*. It represents allegory. Also a term for a Jewish legend.

Ein Sof—Literally, "endless" or "infinite." The highest, unknowable aspect of the Divinity.

Eretz Yisrael—The land of Israel.

Erev Shavuot—Jewish holidays begin in the evening, rather than in the morning. "Erev" means "evening", and "Erev Shavuot" refers to the evening on which the holiday of Shavuot begins.

Galut—The Diaspora.

Gan Eden—The Garden of Eden.

Gehenna—Jewish Hell, where the souls of the wicked are punished for up to twelve months.

Hagigah—A tractate of the Talmud containing discussions about the celestial mysteries.

Hasidim—Members of the Jewish sect begun by the Baal Shem Tov; the disciples of a Hasidic master, known as a Rebbe.

Havdalah—Means literally, separation. The ceremony at the end of the Sabbath separating the Sabbath from the rest of the week.

Huppah—The bridal canopy.

Hazzan—A cantor.

Kaddish—The prayer for the dead. It is required that a son say it for his parents three times a day for eleven months following their death.

Kavanah—Literally, spirit. The spirit, or intensity that is brought to prayer and other ritual, without which it is an empty form.

Kedushah—Holiness.

Kehillah—The Jewish community.

Ketubah—A traditional Jewish marriage contract.

Kippot—Skullcaps worn by religious Jews. (Singular: *Kippah*.)

Klippot—Literally, shells. Fragmentary forces of evil described in the texts of Jewish mysticism.

Lamed Vov Tzaddikim—The 36 Just Men who, according to legend, exist in every generation. By their merit, the generation is sustained.

Ma'ariv—The evening prayer.

Machzor—A prayer book for Jewish festivals.

Mashiah—The Messiah. According to Jewish tradition there will be two Messiahs, Messiah ben Joseph, who will prepare the way, and Messiah ben David, who will bring the End of Days.

Mashumid—An apostate.

Menorah—A seven-branched candelabrum described in the Bible and used in Temple days. There is a special menorah for use for the festival of Hanukah, which has nine branches—one to be lit on each night and one to be used for lighting the others.

Merkevah—Literally, chariot. The chariot in the vision of Ezekiel. Used in Jewish mysticism to refer to a chariot used for heavenly ascents.

Mezuzah—An amuletic case containing a parchment on which prayers are inscribed, appended to every doorway in the house of a religious Jew.

Midrash—A method of exegesis of the biblical text. Also refers to post-talmudic Jewish legends as a whole. A *midrash* (no capitalization, pl. *midrashim*) is an individual legend in the style of *Midrash*.

Midrash Tanhuma—A major midrashic collection based on the books of the Torah, dating from the 9th and 10th centuries.

Minhah—The afternoon prayer.

Minyan—A quorum of ten Jewish males over the age of 13, which is required for a congregational service.

Mitzvah—A Divine commandment. The Torah lists a total of 613 obligations. The word is also commonly used to refer to a good deed. (Plural: *Mitzvot*.)

Modeh Ani—The prayer that is said immediately upon waking. It thanks God for restoring the soul, which dwells on high during sleep, to the body.

Mohel—A person trained to perform circumcision.

Moshel—A parable or tale.

Motze Shabbat—The period at the end of the Sabbath. Traditionally among Hasidim a time of reflection or celebration.

Nekevah—The feminine aspect.

Neshamah—A soul.

Parashah—The weekly portion that is read from the Torah.

Pardes—Literally, "orchard." Also, the Hebrew for "Paradise." As an acronym, its four letters refer to a system of biblical interpretation on four levels: *Peshat, Remez, Drash, Sod.*

Pargod—Literally, "curtain." In Jewish mysticism, it refers to the curtain that is said to hang before the Throne of Glory.

Pesach—The festival of Passover, commemorating the Exodus from Egypt.

Peshat—The first, literal level of biblical interpretation in the four-level system known as *Pardes*. It refers to the plain meaning of the text.

Pilpul—A fine point of the law. Literally, "peppers," to indicate the intricacies of talmudic argument.

Reb—The term commonly used among Hasidim, to address each other, which may be loosely translated as "Mr."

Rebbe—A Hasidic master.

Remez—The second level of the system of biblical interpretation known as *Pardes*. It refers to the use of symbolism.

Schnaps (Yiddish)—Liquor.

Sefer—A book.

Sefer Ezekiel—The book of Ezekiel in the Bible.

Sefer Pardes—A lost book reputed to have been written by Moshe de Leon.

Sefer Raziel—A legendary book said to have been given to Adam by the angel Raziel at God's command. It was believed to have been destroyed along with the Temple in Jerusalem. In the Middle Ages a book by the same title consisting largely of spells, reclaimed the title, and was a common text in many Jewish libraries.

Sefer Yetzirah—An early (8th century) kabbalistic treatise.

Sephardi Machzor—The Sephardic prayer book used for the Jewish festivals, in contrast to the Ashkenazi Machzor, which was more commonly used by the Hasidim.

Shabbos—The Sabbath.

Shahareis—The morning prayer.

Shammes—The sexton of a synagogue.

Shavuot—The festival commemorating the giving of the Torah at Mount Sinai.

Shekhinah—The Divine Presence or Bride of God, also known as the Sabbath Queen. Closely identified with the Jewish people and the city of Jerusalem. Also, the female aspect of God.

Shiur—The time between the *minhah* and *Ma'ariv* services, sometimes utilized as a study session.

Shivhei ha-Besht—(In Praise of the Baal Shem Tov)—The earliest book of the tales of the Baal Shem Tov.

Shofar—The ram's horn that is ritually blown on the High Holy Days.

Siddur—The daily prayer book.

Sod—The fourth level of the four-level system of biblical interpretation known as *Pardes*. It refers to secret or mystical interpretations.

Sopher—A scribe. One who writes holy texts and also records, as they are spoken, the teachings and tales of Hasidic Rebbes.

Tallisim—The prayershawls worn by religious Jews during prayer. (Singular: *tallis*)

Tanach—The Bible. An acronym made up of *Torah*, *Neviim* (Prophets), and *Ketuvim* (Writings).

Tefillin—Phylacteries worn by men over 13 during the daily morning prayers.

Thirteen Principles of Maimonides—Theological systematization composed by Moses Maimonides and recited daily as part of prayer.

Tikkun—Acts of restoration and redemption.

Teshuvah—Repentence. Literally, "return."

Torah—The first five books of the Bible, which, according to Jewish tradition, were given by God to Moses on Mount Sinai. The most sacred books of the Bible for Jews.

Tzaddik—A righteous man, one who has achieved a high level of spirituality.

Tzaddik ha-dor—The leading Tzaddik of his generation.

Tzedakah—Charity/Righteousness.

Urim Ve'Thummim—The oracular breastplate worn by the High Priest in the Temple.

V'hakol Sharir V'kayam—Literally, "It is valid and binding."

Yahrzeit—The yearly observance of the date of a person's death.

Yom Kippur—The most solemn day of the Jewish religious year. The Day of Judgment, in which God is believed to inscribe a person's name in the Book of Life for the coming year, sealing a person's fate.

Yenne Velt (Yiddish)—The Other World, i.e. the world after this life. Also, the realm of angels, spirits, and demons.

Yetzer Hara—The Evil Inclination. An aspect of all human beings.

Yetzer Tov—The Good Inclination. An aspect of all human beings.

Zahar—The masculine aspect.

Zohar—The Book of Splendor. The primary book of Kabbalah, the body of Jewish mystical texts.

Howard Schwartz was born in St. Louis, Missouri in 1945. He attended Washington University, and presently teaches at the University of Missouri-St. Louis. In addition to *Rooms of the Soul*, he is the author of the *The Captive Soul of the Messiah: New Tales about Reb Nachman* and editor of *Gates to the New City: A Treasury of Modern Jewish Tales, Voices Within the Ark: The Modern Jewish Poets* (with Anthony Rudolf), and *Elijah's Violin & Other Jewish Fairy Tales*.

Tsila Schwartz was born in Jerusalem in 1952. She studied art at Hebrew University and has taught art in Israel and the United States. She is a calligrapher who specializes in the writing of *Ketuboth*, Jewish wedding contracts, and traditional Jewish amulets. Her work has been published in magazines and in the book *Elijah's Violin & Other Jewish Fairy Tales*. She also designed the cover of the record *A Festival of Jewish Music*.